I0780759

For you, O Lord,

Come quickly -

...the end thereof...

THE CHURCH AND THE GOSPEL OF DECEPTION

M.W. CAPEHART

"And I will bring the blind by a way that they knew not; I will lead them in paths that they have not known: I will make darkness light before them, and crooked things straight. These things will I do unto them, and not forsake them."

Isaiah 42:16

Table of Contents

Preface

The unfaltering carelessness in dealing with the souls of man in the matter of his salvation, as well as the unadulterated consent to the blatant worldwide corruption of doctrine present in our sanctuaries today, is an unmitigated disaster borne out of the motives and intentions of the unregenerate mind, whose very essence bears the unmistakable and express image of the apostate church.

A confiscated and non-discerning establishment of believers, captive under the control of false teaching and influence of the Evil One, has rendered the Church complicit in leveling the largest broadside attack upon the most sacred of her doctrines Christendom has ever known.

Our compromised accountability to defend her has posited upon our hands the undeniable stain of reproach, and our silence of breath in acknowledgement of our dereliction of duty can never dispel the shame for which we are beset. These are the ways of death and destruction as the wise old proverb so solemnly decrees…

"**There is a way which seemeth right unto man, but the end thereof are the ways of death.**"

Proverbs 14:12

In these last days in this garden of tares, as we witness before our very eyes the collective Bride of Christ partake of the forbidden fruit for which cause her Savior's blood was once shed, we are left only to marvel at our untimely presence of arrival upon this woefully tragic scene.

As we stand on the brink of our mortality in this final chapter and stage of human existence, will the appearance of our courage enrapture us to save her in this fleeting, frozen moment of time, or be swept away with her memory into eternity?

Exhortation

The courage of those who will dauntlessly gaze into the looking glass of self- assessment that this injunction mandates is highly commendable and of utmost necessity. While many who dare tread its pages will be met with unsettling furor, there will be those who will find great solace in its support of their firmly held theological views.

Be forewarned, much of the material found in this boldly written and courageously published work will infuriate many because its content flies directly in the face of traditional perspective, today's standards of church practice, and the ecumenical threat of an arrogant postmodern culture.

Many of the objections outlined in this petition, undoubtedly, oppose the mainstream beliefs and practices of our religious society. Many will deny that such atrocities exist within the confines of their beloved assemblies, and some will even brim over with what they will deem as righteous indignation when confronted by the many indictments outlined in the forthcoming chapters.

The following notice serves as a high caution to those of the common faith, whose current condition of the collective whole is of dire concern.

A misapprehended Gospel and corrupt doctrine are the bane of modern evangelical Christianity. The unchallenged and flagrant display of unenlightened teaching that has perverted the truth of God's Word and has deceived generations of believers continues to permeate our houses of worship week after week.

Many of the damnable doctrines and heresies that have plagued the evangelical community and have forced the true Church into a minority subculture throughout its history are exposed and outlined in a relevant context. Topics that most pastors and teachers avoid due to the imminent threat of occupational hazard, ridicule, isolation, and branding by their critics, not to mention their love for the praise of men more than the praise of God, are also briefly discussed.

Are we, as the Body of Christ, presenting a distortion of the salvation of God? How is it that most believers do not understand how to articulate their faith or lack the confidence to share Christ with others? I contend that the answer centers primarily around the believer's testimony of salvation, or rather, the lack thereof.

Though people are naturally prone to adopt the worldviews of their closest peers to shape and principally guide their systems of belief, how is it that the true Church, which is transformed by the blood of Christ, has been conditioned to accept the adaptation of Christianity that the court of public opinion has idealized? At what point was the rightful division of God's Word exchanged for the forbidden fruit of subjective reasoning? Like a Trojan horse, the tactical deception of the enemy's twisted theology has invaded the unguarded court of the unassuming Church with her eyes wide open.

I am hauntedly reminded of the imminent state of affairs that the kingdom of God would face in this Age when Jesus well foretold this present reality in His discourse of the parable of the Wheat and the Tares.

The intended purpose of this address is to lay bare many of the common spiritual malpractices at work within congregations throughout our land, thinly disguised beneath the veneer of moral decency, ethics, and church tradition; to identify with the untold number of those who conscientiously object to the anthropocentric religion that has invaded the sanctuaries of God's people and ultimately threatens to replace the lamp of our first love; and finally, to call on the elect of God to act with vigilant authority and discernment in reclaiming the role of virtue and influence in the governance of our sanctuaries and secular society that rightly defines the true Church and reassumes the voice of reason, sobriety, and certitude within our communities and culture.

May this admonition serve as a plea for the true Church of God and its leadership to recognize and turn from the error of her careless dealings with the souls of man and her blind devotion to the whims of an almost robotic religious society to finally summon the courage to take a stand against the machine of organized religion.

The devastation that this machine has created lies in the wake of a sinister, man- centered program that, through the power of Satan, has not only desecrated the sanctity of scripture but has perpetuated the subversion of the Church's original conquest.

These practices have existed for generations and continue to be the prevailing commission of the unrealizing evangelical majority.

The tolerance of errant teaching and adoption of corrupt manners equate us with the apostate church of worldliness and spiritual whoredom whom the Lord will ultimately judge.

The enemy is using the apathy of many of God's own people to accomplish his will, and because of our shameful complacence, the fact that the gates of Hell even dare to prevail against the faith that the true Church has been charged so earnestly to contend for blindsides us.

The Army of God is failing to adorn its armor on the battlefield of true soul winning. The banner of indisputable truth, that once flew so proudly among us, has been tattered and war-torn, not by unrelenting pursuit and defense of God's Word, but rather by the agendas of compromised leaders who have facilitated the hijacking and ultimate derailment of sound doctrine that has sabotaged the Church's original mission. Its countenance, reduced to the white flag of tolerant surrender and on the horizon of our indifference, looms the warning that the time of times is, behold, suddenly upon us.

"And through covetousness shall they with feigned words make merchandise of you: whose judgment now of a long time lingereth not, and their damnation slumbereth not." 2 Peter 2:3

A Way That Seems Right unto Man

"...the unveiling of divine truth will always prove to be beyond the realm of what may be fathomed by the finite mind of man, apart from the interceding revelatory operation of the Spirit."

It may surprise you to know that the average evangelical minister today among protestant denominations is presenting a message, gospel, and savior that is utterly skewed and shaped primarily by his worldview. Consequently, this worldview, over time, has become the popular position of the mainstream majority of professing believers today. The assumption of doctrinal positions that have been adopted and put into practice by generations prior, have been largely unchallenged on their merit, yet accepted as the gold standard of incontestable truth for biblical Christianity today. Thus, when a minister's knowledge is built solely upon what he has been taught apart from that which he has confirmed experientially, the product of that knowledge is, at best, a document certifying assent to the theological programming he received from the institution by which his degree was procured. Likewise, the majority of believers who profess Christ in this day and age have merely subscribed to the same indoctrination, only without the credentials to show for it.

The apparent lack of regenerated and discerning, yet otherwise brilliant, minds that have led our theological institutions and congregations for decades, have gradually relented their evangelical ambitions having rather shifted their focus to the art and practice of selling a brand because the seeming paradox in understanding how souls are truly won remains a wonder whose grasp eclipses the recesses of the natural mind and a task for whom the living impaired were never so intentioned.

This phenomenon has resulted in a harvest of tares in the wheatfield of evangelism, and amid this anomaly of confusion, the compromise of the Church to espouse and tolerate a doctrine that violates the very heart and essence of its originator's intent, has been permitted to infiltrate our pulpits and constitutions, triggering, at our own behest, the imminent fallout of what was once known as the Church.

An individual's witness should bear personal testimony in his or her declaration of salvation. The reason that churches today do not witness effectively, or at all, is because there is no testimony or witness within them. 1 John 5:10 makes this clear:

"He that believeth on the Son of God hath the witness in himself:"

Believing on the Son of God, as a cognitive action, is not the means by which we obtain our witness. Rather, the text is declaring a characteristic truth: the evidence of the witness within us serves as affirming proof that we are true believers. It is important to remember that 1 John, like much of the New Testament, is written in this manner because it is addressed to born-again Christians, not to those seeking to become such. The passage highlights the confirming attributes that will manifest in our lives when our witness is a result of the Holy Spirit's regeneration.

When our testimony is a product of free will or "decisional-regeneration" that merely assents to the facts of the Gospel, responds to an invitation to "receive" or "accept" Christ, or allow us to be led through the absurd task of mouthing a "sinner's prayer", then we must realize that we have only agreed with someone else's assessment of how eternal life is secured. Having performed an action that presupposes the approval of God's acceptance, though be it sincere, we at best, have only met a condition for membership into a religious organization, an initiation into a club of the like-minded. Contrary to the powers that be, nowhere, in the proper context of scripture, are any of these methods ever endorsed or substantiated as a path to God, hence the concern for the careless dealing with the souls of man.

Unfortunately, the Gospel-centered preaching of our day, if any, has been relegated to a mere presentation of religious facts and an invitation to accept those facts in an effort to affirm the faith of the majority and appease popular opinion. I mean, who would dare contest the degree-holding meanderings of the preacher's misguided theology? Certainly, not the vulnerable and uninformed who are at the mercy of his trusted authority.

We have taken for granted the salvation of our congregants for so long that more emphasis has been placed upon their continuing development than on the initial evangelistic efforts necessary to see them truly saved in the first place. The emphasis on teaching principles for Christian living to the presumably saved is not only an exercise in futility but is an inexcusable oversight on those called to preach, and because of the prevalence of this progressing reality, masses of individuals throughout history have been led to cling to a salvation for which they have never truly acquired.

We often first learn of the things of God from our parents and intuitively trust their judgment, but God calls each of His children to their own personal walk with Him. We cannot continue to ride the coattails of those we trust and admire simply because we esteem their spiritual adeptness or biblical knowledge to exceed that of our own. It is up to each individual to discover and understand what it is they believe and why, based first and foremost, on a position of a born-again transformation that produces a life of fellowship with God that is sensitive to and under the constant control of the Holy Spirit, a consistent and disciplined habit of the study of God's Word and finally, developmental application of oneself to the real-world challenges to which he will be exposed and face at every angle.

Those who insist on riding the coattails of others are primary targets for Satan, who cannot wait for them to take the bait of a church whose Spirit-less doctrine will not produce a new birth. Instead of being won to the kingdom of God, they're won to a church, which may be, in God's name, doing many wonderful works but is treading the wide path of a faulty evangelism whose doctrine will end in ultimate rejection by the Savior (Matthew 7:22-23).

Many times, throughout my Christian life, I've heard pastors and teachers say that every religion in the world requires that man earn his salvation, but that Christianity is the only religion in the world that does not because God has already done the work for us.

While there is certainly some truth to that assertion, the problem with this statement is that it is always used in a general sense to make a blanket application to the "whomsoever" should choose to "accept" Jesus as their savior. In complete disregard for the context of scripture to fit the classic presumptive narrative, believers completely ignore the fact that they, themselves, voluntarily delve into this very self- imposed toil they preach so adamantly against when they drag their spiritual preconceptions with them into the mix. Man, instinctively and inevitably presumes that reciprocity on his part is necessary to properly consummate such a gift. The wide path of performing actions to merit the approval of God, becomes the course upon which man's natural inclination leads, shifting him ever further down the winding path of religious legalism.

When churches, inadvertently, model this behavior, they are not only blind to the very works-based approach to salvation for which they so vehemently criticize others, they are complicit. When truly saved individuals are lured into this mindset, a "holiness" complex manifests- a relentless pursuit to maintain the righteous appearance upon which one's reputation is predicated at all times. Bear in mind that the regenerate are highly prone to and, to a greater extent, more profoundly impacted by this condition due to the fact that they are operating under the extraordinary energy that a Spirit-filled life endows. While oblivious to this snare, the emphasis of living up to the impossible standards worthy of their new life becomes a feat for which their zeal is ever exhausted.

Examples of this extreme behavior include the compulsion to maintain perfect attendance to every church function, program, or hosted event; over-commitment to volunteer work or ministry service to the point that the original motivation and passion are lost, leaving the individual to go through the motions of formalistic religion because, at some point, the heart is no longer in it, but the standard has been set; all eyes are on the individual and what his peers think becomes more important to him in those moments than what God thinks. While not all believers fall openly victim to this dreadful condition, man's susceptibility to this obvious snare, indeed, presents valid cause for concern.

While expectations are not always imposed verbally by church leaders, the results produced bear the full likeness of strategically engineered coercion tactics. Very often, these impositions are also placed by those outside the believer's religious affiliation. I'm constantly reminded of this and amazed by how much non-believers know and understand what is and isn't acceptable for Christians, even more so than a lot of professing Christians seem to. I believe that in God's infinite wisdom, He foresaw the value in utilizing a great number of the lost and ever-watching world as an accountability measure to help keep His people in check.

For example, somewhere along the way, many seem to have been programmed to fulfill the obligations of an expectant God. It's the "Expectant God Syndrome."

"God expects you to go to church on Sunday," "God expects you to pay your tithes," "God expects you to do this and do that," and the list goes on. These are not statements imagined by lay people. At some point, these ideals were emphasized and made absolute in the minds of the impressionable and likely introduced by overbearing preachers in an effort to obligate and exact unwavering fidelity to the consistent support of their ministries. It must be noted, however, that those who employ these kinds of tactics upon others are only interested in the results they produce. It is the inevitable outcome of the flesh attempting to force the hand of the Spirit and indicative of a way that seems right unto man.

To oblige oneself to a lifestyle that exists only to fulfill the requirements of what one thinks God expects of him, in some effort to appease Him, is a total misapprehension of being "in Christ" and a complete misrepresentation of the personage of God.

The "Christian" life for these people is nothing more than an enduring of religion, and the recipients of this abuse inevitably instill it into the next generation. Fulfilling this religious duty somehow provides a sense of balance, acceptance, and ease of conscience from an empty and otherwise meaningless relationship with God. The Christian life is a list of do's and don'ts that have been passed down from generation to generation, where keeping up appearances was the only way to fit in with those who have been truly transformed. The exciting fellowship in which genuine believers engage must present a great deal of awkward exchange for these pretended sheep who slipped through the gate some other way.

Man's attempt to ascertain, of his own natural ability, the revelatory knowledge of God's Word, along with his claims in understanding the things of the Spirit, have propelled the prideful ambitions of many preachers and teachers. The compelling desire to authoritatively dispense or lord knowledge of any kind over the unlearned and impressionable, especially that of the biblical persuasion, has long since appealed to the ego of man, namely those who have elected themselves to this office as opposed to those whom God has actually called. This unfortunate reality has paved the way for the utter chaos and brotherly discord negatively impacting our ministries. The influx of gross doctrinal error, legalism, and spiritual pride being witnessed in our assemblies today is the result of the withdrawal of the regenerate vigilance that was initially charged to defend the sanctity and reputation of the Church's beliefs. Consequently, this withdrawal has led to the paradigm shift of Christian neutrality that has spawned the identity crisis of the Church in this age.

When a core assembly is comprised of both regenerate and unregenerate believers alike, there will always be an impediment that threatens to stunt the efforts of its mission. When you factor in the often-indifferent career pastor whose self-serving motives take priority over any vision for true growth, a schism is enabled in the Body to persist, allowing what is supposed to be a picture of the

Bride of Christ, to oppose itself. Any potential efforts for progress in this setting are doomed from the outset.

Both groups co-exist to suffer in different ways. The regenerate group, typically under the constant placation of the leadership, subject themselves to continual compromise with the unregenerate in an effort to maintain the unity of the Spirit in the bond of peace, enabling their counterpart unchallenged control and influence. The vexation of the truly elect is the result, yet their fault lies in their failure to vet the testimonies of their elected leaders and members prior to appointment and approval, as well as their neglected ability to maintain the ongoing accountability thereof.

The unregenerate, meanwhile, maintain their position of unchecked authority to co-govern while going through the motions of an empty religion as they have been so enabled. Ever learning yet never able to arrive at the destination of truth.

When truly regenerate believers continue fellowship in these types of assemblies, dissatisfaction and discontent eventually will ensue. As well it should. True Christians are commanded to have nothing to do with the unfruitful works of darkness but rather reprove them (Ephesians 5:11). This includes the fruitless works of false or lazy believers entangled in slothfulness, apathy, procrastination, and indifference, whether in positions of leadership or not. I know this verse intends to define those who are living in gross wickedness, but if God's people fail to vet the testimonies of their congregants and leadership prior to membership and appointment, or neglect to administer the discipline that protects the Church's integrity, they will be liable when the unregenerate rise to the forefront of governance to take the helm as is being witnessed so prevalently in this wicked generation.

Many who have a reputation for godliness often fall prey to the effects of spiritual pride because they are subject to the constant pressure of keeping up appearances while maintaining the expectations of their peers. Corporate prayer is one such area, whether inside the Church or in a public setting, where an individual leading an invocation is enabled to showcase their spirituality, particularly with eloquent and long-winded prayers that usually come off sounding more like a polished performance before the hearers and less like a heartfelt petition before God.

The outward voice of corporate prayer should always be under the direction and conviction of the Holy Spirit and in demonstration of His power, clothed in humility, completely absent of self-promotion and pride. It should also be representative of the honest and genuine demeanor of the individual leading the prayer and serve as an example to the weaker saints as well as the lost, yet as a reminder to those full of conviction that without our righteous standing before holy God, our righteousness would merely aspire to but filthy rags (Isaiah 64:6).

We would do well to heed the point Jesus made in how we should approach the sanctity of prayer. May we, as

God's people, learn to discern reverence from recognition and humility from high regard.

When a believer succumbs to this kind of temptation, his spirituality becomes an inner contest that thrives only to feed his ego. He becomes addicted to the "high" that is experienced when he is acknowledged, recognized, and applauded by others, much like a victim of seductive narcissism.

The perpetual efforts of those who are induced with this incessant desire never miss an opportunity to take advantage of platforms upon which to exhibit their spiritual prowess, including their biblical knowledge, theological adeptness, or emphasis on godly demeanor, constantly campaigning for praise and attention garnered from among their cohorts for their self-righteous exhibitions of model Christianity.

Man is often tempted in this area because his ability to win the approval and praise of others feeds his ego and establishes within him a sense of worth and acceptance. Such behavior, left unchecked by those more mature in the faith, will enable the spiritually proud to self-destruct and potentially posit collateral damage in their wake, leaving others within the congregation disenfranchised. When spiritually mature peers fail to recognize and confront consistent manifestations of spiritual pride in their congregants, they render themselves complicit through their license and enablement. Worse yet, when others begin to buy in and continually praise the individual or pat them on the back, so-to-speak, for their pious performances, the power of the Holy Spirit is quenched, and the ministry's effectiveness is sidelined.

As God's people, may we ever strive to appropriate discernment in our displays of the praise and approval of others.

Most pastors today appear to be oblivious to this phenomenon of spiritual pride in their members and staff, perhaps because they are likely infected with the same condition. Never so near-sighted is anyone than when under the influence of this toxic vexation. It is a cause for concern that threatens to diffuse the effectiveness of any evangelical effort, and church leaders without accountability measures in place will be next to impossible to persuade of having veered off course once encumbered by this ailment.

The Church is only as effective as its most arrogant saint, and without the implementation of wise and godly counsel to keep spiritual pride at bay, the Church will consistently fail to effectively please God in her ministry efforts, and through prolonged neglect, the stage will be set for the inevitability of discouragement, discord, and an invitation for doctrinal dissonance.

As with most any false or spurious teaching, there is usually subtlety in its arrival into the Church. Often, these concepts are esteemed by various leaders, teachers, and lay people within the congregation who inwardly share such views but are kept under the radar until their opportune moment for full disclosure is presented.

While these teachings rarely originate in the minds of those who subscribe to them, they are, however, generally introduced by lay persons of influence from within the fellowship. Usually, such notions are acquired from well-known Bible teachers or popular media sources. Whether or not these personalities are credited for the origin of such ideas, they are certainly accountable for the power of suggestion they ascribe. Bolstered by the endorsement of celebrity and assumed spiritual authority, these fraudulent views can bear an immense weight of influence and control over the impressionable, well-intentioned Bible student.

You will typically notice a change in staff leadership or absence of one or more key members when a subtle new idea or teaching surfaces within the Church. It will usually manifest itself in a small group setting such as a men's or women's Bible study and may lie dormant for weeks or months, nuanced only within the extremities of that group before progressing into a foothold that eventually evolves into a key consensual position suddenly and brazenly supported by the clergy.

One such foothold that likely infiltrated and poisoned the Church in this way is the Lordship Salvation heresy. Lordship Salvation is not always easy to recognize, and proponents of this teaching today rarely refer to it by its name due to the negative connotations it evokes, but surprisingly, there are those who without shame or reservation that proudly will.

Many advocates of this fallacious teaching are merely victims of their own enchantment. The sources who openly promote such ideas that have clearly resonated with and enamored their audiences are in no wise guiltless, but the Church's flock who opt to traipse out beyond the fence to graze on the seemingly greener grass of the pastoral marketplace must know intuitively that they do so at their own peril.

While these kinds of dangerous teachings are subterranean in nature and eventually creep their way into churches through the unchecked diabolical agendas of those Satan uses, the fertile ground of the confused and unregenerate mind is the plow field from which these flowers of evil always stem.

Positions such as these are adopted due to man's inability to grasp the concept of God's gracious revelatory work of salvation through the granted faith and repentance that He alone supplies.

Lordship Salvation is a teaching that presupposes to ensure the affirmation of God's granted gift of eternal life upon man, assuming he has, indeed, truly attained such a gift, by insisting that his salvation bear the hallmarks of a true commitment of obedience to the lordship of Christ.

In a sense, proponents of Lordship Salvation, along with the collective whole of modern-day Christianity, have put the proverbial cart before the horse in that the churches practicing such doctrine have, first of all, disregarded to accurately articulate and ensure the administrative function of regeneration in their teaching, and have rather placed emphasis on conversion living as evidence of a presumed salvation irrespectively. Secondly, the rightful designation of doctrinal terms and their biblically prescribed sequence are contrived. The following outline will serve to tabulate Lordship Salvation's proposed method of salvation:

Faith (man's natural inherent ability to believe)

+

Repentance (man's natural inherent ability to change his mind regarding Christ)

=

Trust (A decision to willingly accept Jesus as Savior)

+

Commitment (A willingness to forsake the world and follow Christ)

+

Submission (A willingness to obey Christ)

=

Genuine Repentance (The result of submission to the obedience of Christ)

=

Salvation, so long as the evidence of commitment and submission remains intact.

One thing proponents of Lordship Salvation have gotten right is the fact that faith and repentance are granted gifts (Ephesians 2:8; 2 Timothy 2:25). Unfortunately, an inadvertent presumption exists within this teaching as well as the majoritarian evangelical host, that asserts that these endowments are somehow inborn in the soul of every individual upon conception. There is a failure at the outset of this teaching to discern and distinguish between the natural ability of man in contrast with the supernatural qualities endowed by God within the salvation sequence. This is the only possible logic that can be attributed to its adherent's misapplication of such key and fundamental doctrines.

Similarly, both groups have failed to articulate and establish that the gift of granted faith is the very substance and installment of the instantaneous regenerative work of God upon the soul and have rather insisted that it is a virtue espoused in the heart of every sinner that can and must be exercised in conjunction with repentance to effect his salvation. However, the very notion of man's volition being imposed upon the sovereign act of God's saving work follows suit with the scripturally unsupported teaching of decisional-regeneration which asserts man's audacious ability to invite himself into the Heaven of God all under the pretense of surrender. Proponents of Lordship Salvation, as others, insist that this allegedly intrinsic faith is somehow a virtue whose applicability falls upon the part of human responsibility, invoking his trust and belief toward a change of mind regarding his inherent rejection of Christ. This faith and repentance exercised unitarily is now tasked with yet another conjunctive requirement, a commitment to be willing to forsake the world as well as a submission to the obedience of Christ to effect a "genuine repentance" which, in the Lordship Salvation equation, constitutes an authentic regenerative experience provided that the purportedly saved individual maintains evidence of said commitment and submission.

Being that genuine repentance, as an assertion by the proponents of Lordship Salvation, comes only on the heels of one's submission to the lordship of Christ makes one question the proponent's understanding of what faith and repentance actually are and how man's employment of these actions to merit the desired outcome are not constituted as "works" by the believing majority. This, unfortunately, mirrors the very reprehensible misapplication of soteriological doctrine for which the Church at large is principally and primarily delinquent and perhaps explains where such a notion likely originated.

Practitioners of this false teaching remain oblivious to the fact that genuine repentance is something produced in the new creature by the solely engineered supernatural conviction of the Holy Spirit, not something that's manufactured on the part of the individual to sway God's mercy to save them. The permission that society has granted popular culture to influence the narration and direction of its theology has only enabled the scourge of ignorance that dominates our existence.

Our faith to believe is granted (Ephesians 2:8-9) by the Lord to His elect. It is not a faculty we possess that bears some hidden virtue that gets the ball rolling. The idea that man's free will or volition is somehow imposed upon God's mercy to save him is completely without scriptural merit and an utter misconstrual of the attributed character qualities God has previously and consistently exemplified throughout history.

While God typically begins His saving work by the Spirit in an individual's life through a courtship-like pursuit of sorts, God's work of regeneration as it pertains to the dynamic transformation of His elect is an event in the salvation sequence that produces an undeniably immediate and instantaneous attitude of genuine repentance in the heart of the individual.

True to Christ's description of how man arrives at this change (John 6:37, 44, 65), it must be inferred that the pursuit of the man formerly known as "Saul" was well underway before God's glory shone round about him on the road to Damascus.

Saul was present (Acts 7:58) and witnessed the preaching of Stephen that utterly rocked the foundations of the Jewish faith. There are notable reactions mentioned in the account that tell us:

> "And they were not able to resist the wisdom and the spirit by which he spake."
>
> Acts 6:10

> "And all that sat in the council, looking stedfastly on him, saw his face as it had been the face of an angel."
>
> Acts 6:15

> "When they heard these things, they were cut to the heart, and they gnashed on him with their teeth."
>
> Acts 7:54

Saul was no doubt impacted by these events. They challenged the very core of his beliefs, which he had only known on an intellectual plane his entire life. Afterward, witnessing the stoning of Stephen (Acts 22:20) as he kneeled down and cried with a loud voice saying, "Lord, lay not this sin to their charge" (Acts 7:60a), merely heartbeats before his death, enough of an impression was left upon Saul that he did not hesitate to disclose the account from his testimony before the Jews (Acts 22:1-21). Bound in their custody, knowing they would likely not receive such testimony, he not only mentioned his encounter with Christ on the road to Damascus, but he also referred to Stephen as a martyr.

Prior to this mock trial in Jerusalem, Saul, who would later become Paul, was in transit, zealously carrying out the very duties of his religious convictions in his continued persecution of Christians. It must be understood that Saul's subsequent transformation on the road to Damascus instantly produced a God-engineered, genuinely repentant heart of obedience, and the fruit produced in his life was not merely accomplished by fulfilling religious obligation but by the power of the Holy Spirit working in and through him.

As it is with all regenerated persons, obedience to the Spirit became his daily response and highest priority. Though living in obedience to the Spirit was a choice he had to make each day, Paul understood that much like he was no longer bound to live by the letter of the Mosaic law, neither was his salvation conditioned upon his perfect ability to maintain that obedience. Paul's discourse in Romans 7 underscores this truth in his conclusive recognition that while his sinful nature would always be at war within him, his position in Christ would trump any failure that could ever impede that ability. This fact is further substantiated by the scriptural account we have on record of Paul's repeated disobedience to the Lord's command not to return to Jerusalem, which led to the finality of his commission (Acts 13:2,47; 21:4; 22:17-21). The Lord illustrates evidence of this truth when He later stood beside Paul in a prison cell and spoke to him, signifying that He would never forsake him:

"Be of good cheer, Paul: for as thou hast testified of me in Jerusalem, so must thou bear witness also at Rome." **Acts 23:11**

Clearly, God commands obedience from His elect, but just as His free gift of salvation does not constitute the absurd notion of a spiritually dead man's ability to exercise it prior to his salvation, neither is our salvation predicated upon our ability to perfectly maintain that obedience, but only by His grace. (Ephesians 2:8-9).

Paul's experience on the road to Damascus demonstrates how lordship is something that is acquired the moment we are personally encountered by the stark reality of the holiness of God, not something that has to be learned and then put into practice. It is an instantaneous and automatic response to God's work of regeneration by the Spirit.

Paul's first and immediate instinct to this revelation that Jesus is God was to inquire what He would have him do (Acts 9:6). This immediate submission to the authority of Christ is the example we have on record of Lordship 101 and is an unmistakable picture of how obedience and lordship not only go hand in hand but is the undeniable product of God's effective regeneration.

It must be noted that our best attempts to please God through our obedience prior to salvation are not only nonsensical, but they are also altogether impossible.

"As it is written, There is none righteous, no, not one: There is none that understandeth, there is none that seeketh after God. They are all gone out of the way, they are together become unprofitable; there is none that doeth good, no, not one."

Romans 3:10-12

The reason that newly converted individuals fail to consistently exhibit the long- term fruits of true repentance, obedience, or the likeness of Christ in their walk is because they have attempted to procure their salvation through the method of self- conversion tactics.

They have converted their thinking to trust, accept, and adopt a set of beliefs and teachings but have not experienced the transforming power of the Spirit of God that, alone, is responsible for generating this conversion.

The repentance that the Lord calls us to is not simply a change of mind but rather is a commanding call by the Spirit, designed to evoke a response in an individual through His supernatural work in the hearts of those ordained to eternal life. It is a revelation of God's person to an individual, leading to a response where our spirit bears witness with His Spirit, as cited in Romans 8:16.

"It is the spirit that quickeneth; the flesh profiteth nothing: the words that I speak unto you, they are spirit, and they are life." **John 6:63**

This action, initiated solely by the Lord (Ephesians 2:1,4-6,10), instantaneously infuses the new creation with an enormous and unrelenting ability to submit to His obedience, supernaturally empowering an unwavering commitment to the lordship of Christ. It's not that the individual can't or won't ever fall into sin, but that the transformative experience of regeneration he has undergone can never be revoked. The only way one could ever aspire to such a plane is through the omnipotent power of the indwelling and never- forsaking Holy Spirit of God.

For a regenerated believer, the Lordship Salvation teaching, at first, might be construed as seemingly harmless because that it appeals directly to the heart of true, well-meaning Christians, who, by virtue of their transformation, would naturally place a high reverence on the lordship of Christ anyway. However, its destructive element lies in its primary insistence that every believer must express a life of devotion to the lordship of Christ based on elements of the Gospel of the kingdom, asserting that God's granted repentance is acquired upon one's subsequent submission to that lordship, totally corrupting the Gospel message of Grace. Advocate's ineptitude to discern the Gospel of Grace from the Gospel of the kingdom stands in contrast as one of their most damning shortfalls.

I am not discounting the importance and necessity of living a life of devotion to the lordship of Christ by any means, but rather I am calling attention to the error of the teaching's definition and application of doctrinal terms, its estimation of salvific order, its obvious failure to discern between the specific commands of the Church and Israel as well as correctly differentiate the dispensational distinctions thereof.

The Bible is very clear in its teaching that man does not make a consensual decision to initiate salvation (John 1:12-13; 3:3; 6:37,44,65; Romans 3:10-12; 8:7), and that lordship is the natural response of a transformed life (Acts 9:6; John 9:35-38), not the means to one. The individual practicing this brand of Christianity has been deceived into adding his works of righteousness to an irrevocable redemption, assuming the individual has, indeed, truly been saved; otherwise, he or she is living out a simulated walk with God, climbing an impossible ladder to Heaven that will never breach the height of the ceiling.

Those truly regenerated who are entangled in this teaching have failed to understand the concept and nature of their transformation. In their failure to acknowledge this fact, although maintaining the godliest of intentions, the tendency to bequeath these same expectations of lordship or other unvetted beliefs upon their peers presents an outcome whose likelihood is of inevitable probability.

The insistence that people, in their own power, must demonstrate total reverence for, devotion to, and repentance toward God as an insuring contingency of their salvation is a complete undermining of the Scriptures as well as the authenticating work of the Spirit.

Advocates of Lordship Salvation insist that *sinners* must exercise faith in conjunction with repentance to effect the regenerative process, which is misaligned with the biblical doctrine of Total Depravity, yet adherents rightly attribute the entire work of salvation to God - an unobscured distinction of glaring contradiction.

Because the presumed power of the self-summoned faith of unregenerate man as well and his self-ascribed repentance is non-effectual in producing the New Birth, the possibility for him to utilize both "virtues" in conjunction with total submission and commitment to effect his salvation, as so prescribed, presents a feat of shear impossibility. When coupled with the consideration that unregenerate man is born spiritually dead in sins and trespasses (Ephesians 2:1), how a spiritual corpse then possesses the ability to exercise any of these allegedly inborn faculties is beyond the sensibility of practical theology or even common sense.

This is a great example of ministries who cite the cherry-picked absolutes of scripture to substantiate their doctrinal beliefs and statements of faith, yet in application, the methods actually being practiced prove to be wildly inconsistent and profoundly contradictory of the published views they so staunchly express.

Lordship Salvation appeals to the unregenerate because it fits the unchecked theological narrative of decisional-regeneration, and the evidentiary support insisted upon by their cohorts regarding their salvation lies simply in the individual's ability to maintain the appearance thereof, precluding an actual testimony of genuine transformation as is the custom of so many who profess Christ. It's a practice imposed upon the acceptor of Jesus that serves as a counterbalance for the "easy-believism" that its advocates so vehemently criticize. The requirement of walking the straight and narrow path becomes the price paid for the salvation assumed and serves to ensure the authenticity of the subscriber's conversion and obedience in the eyes of its leadership, enabling leaders to maintain a measure of oversight and accountability of the adherent's ongoing submission and commitment to the faith in perpetuity.

The Lordship Salvation adherent's incessant overemphasis in requiring authenticating evidence of the salvation and devotion of others based on these imposed requirements is a self-inflicted overcompensation of concern.

Giving the benefit of the doubt by understanding that the intention is likely based on pure and honest motives, it is at the great expense of the souls of man and the subversion of the sound and systematic theology of the Scriptures for which we, the Church, must never stand.

The resolute infiltration of this teaching into the Church should give pause for and grave concern of its consequential threat to our God-given commission, deserving the full penalty of swiftly executed justice in the immediate forcible eviction of its agency without controversy or respite.

The emphasis on the necessity of discipleship living prior to regeneration is nothing short of an unnecessary lading of undue burden upon a prospective believer by the Church, intended to convince her leaders that an individual is prepared for the saving work of God's effectual grace. Once again, man, in his consolation to ensure the salvation of others for his own appeasement, he does what the religious have always done; he adds something to the sufficiency of God's supernatural provision.

The religious leaders of the Old Testament, as well as in Jesus' day, were constantly adding and imposing their conditions upon the law in an effort to tidy up and make sure their God given rules suited and appeased their self-righteous standards. If the fulfillment of the conditions of discipleship were truly a mandate that the prospective believer must meet prior to his salvation, it would be a consideration no one would ever choose and a criterion for which none would ever qualify. The challenge Jesus gave to his disciples to take up their crosses, deny themselves, and follow Him would clearly point to a decision we would make of our own volition instead of a work invoked by the Holy Spirit.

The expectation of the unregenerate to autonomously assess whether or not the cost justifies the means in following a Jesus whom they have not known, experientially or otherwise, by order of the subjugating Church, is not only an outrageous implausibility on her part but is a preconceived overestimation of the unregenerate's ability to ever logically arrive at such a conclusion.

Now consider the immense barriers of those who possess completely different languages and cultures coming to this logic and the unnecessary futility of effort that has been attributed to the missionary cause by a misapprehended doctrine. However the Gospel has been presented in these endeavors, it is more likely than not that the path to Heaven has been addressed in 1 of 2 ways: "Make a Decision" (easy- believism) or "Count the Cost " (lordship emphasis/works). Regardless, the fact is we have financed missionary endeavors all over this planet for centuries that emulate what the collective Church has historically believed and practiced, and based on the yield of these approaches, it has become painstakingly obvious that something is amiss.

The emphasis and demands of discipleship upon a prospective believer prior to the work of the Spirit is not only an insult to the intelligence of the Church, which is made in God's image but is equally insulting to the biblical process of soteriology. The Holy Spirit equips us *only* at the moment of our New Birth with every necessary desire needed to grow in faithfulness and maturity. It is not based on the logic and ideologies of anthropocentrism. God does not choose us based on the preselected options we offer Him as prospective candidates; He effectively equips all those He calls.

These elements, accentuated by the Church as a necessary component of affirming one's salvation, are nothing more than a tactic engineered by man with the intention of authoritatively policing her obedience and assuaging the unsettling truth that man does not control his own destiny, introducing a narrow and misleading path into a maze of error, confusion, and entrapment.

Anyone who has ever claimed to be regenerated under the Lordship Salvation model, whether they realize it or not, was saved despite this approach, not because of it. Any truly saved person's honest effort to diligently apply themselves to aptly understand this truth would certainly arrive at this conclusion. The Holy Spirit is the primary and only onboard accountability partner that God, in His infinite wisdom, ever equipped man with to insure his obedience and submission.

To place additional burden atop that which, from the outset, is already impossible for man to acquire on his own not only exposes the sheer ignorance and blatant disregard for the rightful division of God's Word by those who insist on employing such measures but reveals man's narcissistic tendency to rule and control the outcomes and fortunes of others. This is either the work of the honestly misinformed or the cruel intentions of malicious and sinister defectors.

The imposition of conditions that hinge upon one's salvation is one of the oldest tricks in the book. The Judaizers of the early Church in the Book of Acts chapter 15 were guilty of subscribing to this same practice by their insistence of invoking circumcision upon believing Gentiles.

The "Author of Confusion" is no misnomer. The ability to cast doubt in the minds of God's people is the first lesson scripture teaches us about our enemy. He doesn't always use the ill-intentioned. The best lie is the one that sounds most like the truth. Satan knows this and many times uses God's own people to do his bidding. If he can convince church leaders to endorse a brand of logic that sounds like the truth, then what more effective source to further his objective?

Nothing sounds more natural to a saved person than taking up his cross and following Jesus. It is the least and most natural thing any new, unassuming child of God could ever hope to do. Expecting an unregenerate individual to do the same, however, would likely draw the blank stare that I'm sure at least one of the disciples must have had on their face when Jesus asked them to take up theirs.

However, there are those who, for the promise of Heaven, are willing to give it a go. Sadly, the Church has unduly taken the liberty to pronounce eternal life upon many who, in reality, remain in an unregenerate state, those who truly and presently possess no such hope yet are charged with living up to and fulfilling these otherwise impossible standards as a condition of securing the promise of Heaven.

While no born-again Christian would argue that God has called all His children to live a holy life, the gall of church leaders to ill-advisedly levy such burden upon the backs of the lost is abhorrent and inexcusable. The problem for many is that they become entangled in this teaching after having been saved, making their disencumbrance all the more improbable due to their unwavering loyalty and allegiance to the Almighty Church to whom they've so admirably indebted and devoted themselves.

This is why it is imperative that a truly saved individual walking with God not only allow the fellowship of the Holy Spirit to maintain control of their daily life but surround themselves with wise, godly counsel for insight, accountability, and perspective, as well as continually saturate their heart and mind in the Word of God. Not merely in a routine of basking in the awe and wonderment of the Spirit's presence but diligently applying themselves to wisdom, knowledge, and the understanding of truth.

For some time now, churches have reimagined the concept of discipleship to suggest a more formidable use of it as an evangelistic tool. The commission of Paul to Timothy to commit to faithful men who shall be able to teach others, the things that Timothy had heard of Paul among many witnesses, has now been redefined to suggest embodying the successful image of the business-minded disciple leader. Not in any real effort to evangelize the lost and teach them to live Christ-honoring lives or even provide effective oversight of church plants, but rather to ensure they emphasize to their recruits the importance of dressing for success, standards of hygiene, professional demeanor, pitch delivery, follow- up, and closing the deal. "Christians ought to look successful", I heard one preacher say. It gave me pause to consider which gospel he was selling, but after I heard his "evangelistic" spill, my heart cringed, and it became excruciatingly obvious that the Jesus of the Bible was far from it.

The number of books on this reformulated version of discipleship that have been endorsed by leaders to aid in their failing attempts to grow their dead churches is bewildering. Much of this can be attributed to the insurgence of leadership and self- help books that flooded the Christian retail market at the turn of the new millennium. This is the era that truly capitalized on the business of "doing church" that continues to this day and is the epitome of the secular emergent worldview that has led the Church to essentially condense her evangelistic efforts and presentation of the Gospel message into a multi-level marketing sales pitch.

As a means to exponentially increase their ranks, because leaders can't seem to figure out why their approach to doing God's work has fallen flat on its face, churches have resorted to a strategy of secular business tactics whereby members are conditioned to recruit and coerce others who will, in turn duplicate the process. While, in theory, this approach may resemble the biblical discipleship model, it is merely an adaptation and compromise of true Christian ethics, the very essence of the flesh attempting to lead the Spirit.

Man's logic in employing a strategic model of evangelistic stewardship is one thing, but it's the blind devotion of the Church, in whose clutches the souls of man continue to be carelessly dealt with, operating at an increased rate of intensity to satisfy her determination to expand the kingdom at any cost that is most disconcerting. Blind leaders pronouncing eternal life upon the lost, then grooming them to clone others, is the product of the otherwise well-intentioned ways of man whose end will always and ultimately result in death and destruction.

The emphasis on discipleship is always coupled with another major misapplied practice: the observance of water baptism. In fact, the church at large has instituted this practice and insists that it remains a biblical ordinance. The last time I checked, there is only one ordinance that the Lord ever instituted that is still applicable for this dispensation- the commemoration of His Last Supper until He returns.

Though a clear understanding of scripture will refute such a notion, once an entity as large as the post-apostolic era of Christianity, which by the way, was largely dominated and controlled by Catholicism, has imposed such an ordinance, who would dare contest the validity of such a practice so widely honored and revered?

With most of us Christians understanding just about enough scripture to get ourselves into a theological stumper, it is not hard to imagine the susceptibilities we are prone to in misconstruing many critical components of God's Word that assume the applicability of various implied commands.

While the command to "Go ye therefore and make disciples of every nation, baptizing them…." was an action item that Jesus commissioned His disciples to undertake, Jesus was well aware of the changes that would unfold after Pentecost once the Holy Spirit was unleashed upon the Church, meaning that while the heart of this directive has a place of honor, reverence, and some degree of applicability among the Bride of Christ, this commission, that the Church has collectively taken upon herself to fully mandate to its congregants, is, in part, dispensationally out of context and without rationale.

The record of account we have is found in the Book of Acts chapter 15, notably in reference to Paul and Barnabus' encounter with the Church in Jerusalem, where believing Pharisees desired to exact upon believing Gentiles the need to be circumcised. Upon addressing the matter, the apostles arrived at the realization and united conclusion that the imposition of additional requirements upon regenerated Gentiles as a means to ensure their salvation was incongruent with prior revelation received by the apostles and therefore regarded as unnecessary.

The Book of Acts merely records the events or "acts" of the apostles during the time from Jesus' ascension to the inauguration of the Church at Pentecost based on the Spirit's work through the facilitated preaching of the Lord Jesus as well as the accounts of the missions that the Apostle Paul established during that period. It is a record of the transitional period of the birth of the Church that contains dispensational elements that are attributed to specific groups of people at specific times. Just as the temporary use of the miraculous signs and wonders performed by the apostles for God's ordained purpose as a testimony to unbelieving Jews, the means by which individuals first received the Holy Spirit was, indeed, also that of a transitory nature.

In the Book of Acts, chapter 11, after thousands of water baptisms having been performed, we have the account of Peter's recollection and subsequent realization of God's predetermined dispensational plan for the Gentile Church - the Bride of Christ:

"Then remembered I the word of the Lord, how that He said, John indeed baptized with water; but ye shall be baptized with the Holy Ghost."

"Forasmuch then as God gave them
the like gift as He did unto us, who believed on the
Lord Jesus Christ; what was I, that I could
withstand God?" Acts 11:16

Not only was Peter realizing for the first time that this work of the Church was now inclusive of the Gentiles, but also the "ordinance" of water baptism and practice of laying on of hands would no longer be the necessary means by which people would receive the Holy Spirit. God was revealing that the power of preaching Jesus, apart from these prior initial requirements, was now and would hereafter be the primary means by which the Holy Spirit would be received.

As far as water baptism is concerned in the Bible, it is never again mentioned as a necessary function for the Gentile Church or a prerequisite for receiving the Holy Spirit, also known as regeneration, but is referred to only as the figurative spiritual cleansing act of God upon the believer.

Church leaders' continued determination to mandate this non-contextual and misapplied observance upon its members not only underscores man's ignorance of its origins in dispensational applications but also serves to disrobe his ulterior motive to repurpose this once-relevant institution. The place of water baptism in the Church of this era has assumed a new function as a ritualistic initiation for membership into a religious organization and insisted on as a God-ordained command of obedience. One simply answers "yes" to Jesus, is dunked, splashed, or sprinkled, and "Walla!" you're in. Realization of the alarming truth that the local church is not who Christ is coming back for ought to give pause to those who have placed their eternal hopes in their fulfillment of these ill-enforced requirements.

The Church justifies this continued observance of water baptism by quantifying it as "an outward expression of an inward change", insisting that it remains an ordained and acceptable practice for today rather than recognizing and acknowledging it as the inapplicable and unwarranted tradition that it has become. The abuses of this "ordinance" are numerous, but the greatest abuse lies in the fact that the majority who champion this tradition will be those who will continue to flagrantly and irresponsibly pronounce eternal life upon any who buy into the teaching and are convinced of its necessity.

Each baptism showcases an individual's public subscription to the doctrinal persuasion of a given church's theology, presenting an opportunity for that church to garner relevance in the eyes of its community, all to the satisfaction of its ego and reputation. Churches are so desperate for this validation that they will baptize practically anyone who says "yes" to Jesus, regardless of any transformative evidence or testimony of a genuine salvation experience.

Water baptism, in and of itself, is not so much the problem but rather the Church's continued neglect and gross indifference to the Scriptures that pertain to her misapprehension of key doctrines and failed administration of soteriological implements. Nonetheless, the emphasis on following antiquated ordinances and traditions, as well as the seeming lack of concern in her failure to edify herself on eternity hinging matters, is nothing short of an ecclesial travesty.

Regardless of clear and incontrovertible evidence, man is a creature of habit that is going to believe and practice that which he has been programmed, and because he is a prisoner of the beliefs and traditions to which he has been so accustomed, the mere thought of deviation from such is subverted by the consequence of embedded superstition underscoring the reality that the unveiling of divine truth will always prove to be beyond the realm of what may be fathomed by the finite mind of man, apart from the interceding revelatory operation of the Spirit.

May the cry of our hearts bring about an awakening from this trance-induced beguiling which has so captivated the Church, that the ministry of our commission may revive and triumph to a place of acceptance and

honor worthy of her Savior for the sake of all those who
will love His appearing.

The Lost Meaning of Regeneration

"Recognizing that salvation has never been about a choice that man must make, but is the exclusive external work that God performs upon the soul, should grant us resolve as the Church to more closely align ourselves with this facilitative operation of the Spirit, and serve as a caution to never again deviate from it in our preaching."

It is because of man's high regard for education in the role of pastoral leadership that lay persons tend to overtly entrust the more trivial and complex doctrines that intimidate them to the pastor as opposed to taking the responsibility for educating themselves. After all, it's his duty, right? Isn't this why the pastor is entrusted to this office? Sadly, this is the common attitude of most churchgoers, and it is tragically unfortunate. You would think that as much time and money as people invest in their spiritual health by attending church, Bible study, and Sunday school, they might at least consider acquiring and retaining as much of that knowledge as they possibly can. Rather than the members of the Church standing firmly in unified solidarity on the basic knowledge and understanding of their doctrines and practices, many accept that such matters are of an extrinsic nature that exists apart from the two parties. A congregation that isn't sensitive to diligently protecting their beliefs is a prime target for an ungrounded or ill-motivated religious leader to turn them out of the way of sound teaching and, perhaps, lead them down a precarious path of deception and spiritual abuse.

It is vitally important that Church members closely examine, inventory, and reaffirm the doctrines of their faith, practices, and beliefs so that they never find themselves at the mercy of authoritatively dispensed misguided theology. She will also be better equipped to make decisions based on a consensus of core fundamental beliefs and constitutional principles rather than rely on intuition, preference, or external influence. Therefore, it behooves the Church to take these precautionary measures to protect herself, making her confession sure. The pastor holds a position of high regard, but the born-again members are the governing body that elects its pastors and what essentially comprises the nexus of divine facilitation within the Church.

The most defining and necessary qualifications required for the determination and appointment of a pastor should be that he is clearly filled with the Holy Spirit, possesses a sound personal testimony of salvation, has a firm grasp of the Scriptures, rightly able to divide the Word of truth, and his calling by God is evident in his preaching.

At some point, "so-called" members of the Body of Christ settled and elected to appoint those who did not possess these qualities- leaders who obviously never understood the primary purpose of the office, which is to expose every man's need of a Savior by declaring the deity of Christ in their preaching and by their own example of a transformed life, confront the people with the truth of the Gospel message.

Bringing the increase and yielding results is clearly God's job, but effective planting requires good seed, pure water, and faithful plowing by committed farmers with unswerving tenacity and unblemished integrity; ordained, anointed, and specifically called by God. This involves the primary emphasis and direct responsibility of facilitating the work of the Spirit by preaching the Lord Jesus.

"...for there is none other name under heaven given among men, whereby we must be saved." Acts 4:12

Unfortunately, somewhere along the way, the voices of God's witnesses have been muted by a counterfeit group of believers leading the charge with their own agenda, one that has subsequently kicked the Church's constitution to the curb along with her evangelical aspirations, leaving an untold number of true believers disenfranchised and displaced.

As a result, any pastor nowadays who would dare challenge the status quo by exposing the Church's oblivion to that which is biblically apparent to some, would be ostracized and forcibly cast out for the embarrassment that would utterly shame the majority's reputation. However, like many politicians, there are generations of career pastors who have succumbed to the pressures of bureaucracy and have forfeited their ambitions of making a difference, rather having found opportunity in the traditions of their stakeholders to make an easy dollar instead.

I believe that pastors are mostly well-intentioned, but naively misguided presuppositions have often left their fair share of them in the wake of disillusion. The idea that preachers ought to cater to the whims of the congregation is preposterous, but it has become the unconscious norm for any prospective minister who ever expects to retain a position on the church's staff.

The first challenge he will likely face is the immutable reality that compromise will be perpetually on the table, and at the expense of principle and conviction forever hanging in the balance, only the relentlessly shrewd and steadfast will be able to successfully navigate the ebbs and flows of church politics and manage to efficaciously have his honor, commission, and self-respect remain intact. Conversely, if he fails to stand and succumbs to the pressure, he must surely understand that the machine he initially allowed to malfunction at the beginning will most certainly be the system that glitches and devours him in the end.

Ambition must ever learn that disenchantment is often found in the establishment of building the things of God. The flesh simply cannot lead the Spirit. The Spirit must lead the flesh, and without revelation, there can be no transformation.

While holding all experiences up to the standard of scripture as the litmus test by which we are all affirmed or denied, may the affirmed be so bold as to tread the course of the beloved Apostle Paul as he declared the surety of his encounter when he said:

"But when it pleased God, who separated me from

my mother's womb and called me by His grace,

To reveal His Son in me, that I might

preach Him among the heathen; immediately I

conferred not with flesh and blood: Neither went I

up to Jerusalem to them which were apostles before

me; but I went into Arabia, and returned again unto Damascus." Galatians 1:15-17

Paul did not need confirmation or validation from religious leaders or any other authority. He knew whom he had believed (2 Timothy 1:12) and by the historical account we have of his life, he was persuaded even unto death. Every minister knows that there is safety in the multitude of counselors (Proverbs 11:14; 24:6), but Paul was not advocating a renegade approach to religious matters here; he was clearly exercising obedience to a direct commission. His experience was confirmed by the disciple Ananias in the Book of Acts, chapter 9:10-17.

It doesn't matter if we can read, write, speak, or understand Hebrew, Greek, or Aramaic; the primordial language of the Bible is still the language of the Holy Spirit, and without the aid of the Spirit, our understanding will be unfruitful. The subverting of the hearers through the preaching of the Word is the mysterious work of the

Spirit (1 Corinthians 1: 17-21). It is not the eloquence or persuasion of man that convinces the hearers, nor is it in his attempt to methodically dissect and expound the Scriptures (1 Corinthians 2:1-5). Until churches and pastors understand the Apostle Paul's acknowledgement of this reality, which applies to all of God's chosen messengers, every evangelical effort will be an effort that is wasted; efforts that will never truly produce spiritual transformation.

Whether an individual accepts the *general* revelation of God's existence or not is merely a matter of extrapolating that which any logical person could conclude on their own.

Rather, in person or historically speaking, the fact is that God has manifested Himself, not only through the person of Jesus Christ but through His creation for all the world to see (Romans 1:20; Psalm 19:1). Either an individual has personally experienced the saving revelation that only God's Spirit can effect or they quite simply have not.

"For the kingdom of God is not in word, but in power." 1 Corinthians 4:20

Many are the entitlements in this life that man presupposes for himself, and making a decision that will provide eternal security is certainly one of them. Making a decision for Christ is a no-brainer, considering the alternative, and remains the preferred modus operandi for present-day evangelism. With this logic in mind, it makes one truly wonder how anyone could be opposed to the concept of Heaven and Hell. A no-risk eternal life insurance policy with nothing to lose and everything to gain? It would take a special kind of idiot to refuse such an offer and that's exactly what Satan wants you to think.

This, unfortunately, is what is being presented to the interested seeker. This belief holds complete and utter disregard for the context and sacredness of scripture and is purely a method borne out of man's attempt to control his own destiny. The fact that the majority of evangelistic efforts to promote the Gospel have been reduced to presenting the ridiculous notion of making a decision for Christ, which is, by and large, the mainstream consensus of this era, is detestable and is a tactic sourced straight from the playbook of Satan, himself.

Many are the souls upon which eternal life has been erroneously pronounced. The number of individuals who consider themselves born-again Christians simply because they have accepted and followed the in the traditions and practices set forth by their religious predecessors is unconscionable. These are those who have made a conscientious decision to invite themselves into the Heaven of God under the guidance and direction of their spiritual leaders with total disregard or knowledge of the necessary work of the Spirit in the equation.

Our salvation is not predicated on whether or not we assent to the beliefs imposed upon us to "accept" that Jesus is Lord and Savior. Jesus *is* Lord and Savior whether we "accept" Him or not, but our salvation is effected only by the revelatory work of the Spirit, which He and He alone can initiate. It is this personal encounter with His presence that settles the matter of faith once and for all in an individual's life, and without this supernatural revelation, there will be no genuine transformation, and without a genuine transformation, our faith and understanding aspires to but mere speculation and consequent self-delusion.

The idea that eternity has been secured for these people is based entirely upon a misrepresentation of the Scriptures. The individual is misled into believing that he is making great strides toward the approval and acceptance of God's wide-open arms but is, at best, only securing membership into a religious outfit disguised as a life insurance policy with claims no earthly man could ever broker. It is a pretense that provides the claimant with a peace of mind that expires the moment they depart from this life with the exception of the required "soul" deductible.

At some point, man must realize that what he believes has no bearing on the truth. This truth, divine truth, is, was, and ever shall be the living Word of God

(John17:17). It is the only truth that has or ever will stand the test of time. It is non-subjective and reason-free from our views and opinions. It stands alone and is not conditioned by anything we can impose upon it. Its irrefutability is not contingent upon our acceptance of it, nor does the burden of proof regarding its infallibility fall upon itself. It is the measure of faultlessness by which all creation is scaled, and it is the standard by which all living things will be judged (John 12:48). It, alone, has the power to open the eyes of the blind as well as impair the vision of the seer.

Jesus said, "You must be born-again". This was not an action item for Nicodemus. It was simply Jesus' response regarding Nicodemus' failure to understand His mission. One does not simply "accept" Jesus into his heart and acquire eternal life. Contrary to popular belief, nowhere in scripture is this advised or prescribed as a means for man to enter into fellowship with God, but rather through a new birth. Just as man had no say when his physical life began, he is solely at the mercy of God's gracious sovereign plan to effect this transformation.

While man certainly has the ability to choose right or wrong, good or evil, the fact is that man's freedom to choose eternal life was exhausted for all mankind in the Garden of Eden. We are all born under the curse and are not simply free from its edict based on our decision to ignore it or will to believe otherwise.

In terms of spirituality and as it was in Eden, free will only comes into play in the life and mind of one who is already saved. Only a saved individual faces decisions he must make daily in devotion to the guidance of or in opposition to the Holy Spirit, but man's ability to assume his righteous standing based on a determination of right living is entirely a works-based salvation founded on the inherited theology of a religious, yet unenlightened era.

The unregenerate man can impose his free will all he wants in his quest to earn Heaven, but his efforts are futile and will only leave him hoodwinked in the end. The assumptions man makes based on the decisions he has made in his unregenerate state are without substance or virtue. Man, realistically, cannot assume or claim any declared promise of the Word of God under his, otherwise, eternal condition of total depravity. Man is born dead in sins and trespasses (Ephesians 2:1). The Bible is abundantly and emphatically clear on this subject. However awfully ignored this principal doctrine, its immutable and indelible truth cannot be undone or erased.

The faith required for salvation is granted, not claimed or imposed upon the mercy of God. Man's inability to see this is typical of his fallen nature. I suppose it is the reason that he will go to inexhaustible lengths to try and earn the favor of God based on his merits.

The fact is, we don't initiate the New Birth; we have no control over its inception, nor could we sustain its effectual power. It is an occurrence initiated solely by the supernatural power of God, culminating in a confrontation with His holy convicting presence. It is a miraculous event in one's life, should one ever experience it, hence the term "born-again". It is completely a work of God by grace through the granted faith that He alone supplies (Ephesians 2:8).

The New Birth bears similarities with the physical in that its conception is a one- time event and that a gestational period seems to take effect whereby God begins His pursuing work of attraction in an individual's life. This gestational period, though, is realized only in retrospect of the regenerative process, however, it is during this period that God is cultivating this newly conceived faith and desire whereby He draws the individual to Himself, which effectively crescendos, in a moment of time of God's choosing, into a single metamorphic transformation.

God conceives this fundamental work of faith in an individual's life upon His terms and timetable, a faith that will set him on a path to eventually come to know Him as Savior and Lord. It is during this gestational period that the individual begins to acknowledge and develop a desire to know God more intimately.

Many individuals experience a time of personal crisis when this faith begins to germinate, magnifying their desperate need for Divine intervention. In type, personal crises bear some correlation with the anxiety and pangs of the labor process experienced by the mother during childbirth.

As such, the individual, at some point, is faced with an intensified realization of his need for God, a need which, ultimately, will be met the moment he encounters the divine apprehension of God's holy presence. It is at this moment that the individual's granted faith is spawned by the Holy Spirit into a new creation.

As a newborn child could never reject its mother, this confrontation is one that entirely wins his heart, life, and soul and is fully and irresistibly embraced by the individual. It is a sovereign work of God's Holy Spirit initiated and fulfilled completely by Him. And as an unborn child in its mother's womb has no control over its beginning, development, or time of birth, God alone is responsible for the entire work of generating and regenerating life.

The New Birth is not just the transformation of our status, but the transformation of our soul; our mind, our will and emotions being regenerated and sustained by the indwelling Spirit of God (2 Corinthians 5:17). Our mind is transformed because we receive the mind of Christ, our will is transformed evidenced by the sudden change of our desires in no longer pursuing our own selfish lusts, and our emotions are transformed evidenced by the new behavior infused within us by His divine nature, of which we have partaken. This is not to imply in any way that the old nature has departed, but rather, the individual is now indwelled with the aid of God's Spirit that makes all things new.

The fundamental work of faith that God grants His newly begotten has now blossomed and will require constant nourishment for its essential ongoing health, which is provided by the eternal guidance of the indwelling Spirit of God in the individual's life.

Just as a newborn baby immediately craves the bond of his mother's nurturing touch and desires to be fed by his mother's milk, the newly saved individual's automatic and instantaneous response is reciprocated, appropriated, and affirmed by the acknowledgment of his sin under the convicting power of the Holy Spirit, his subsequent repentant heart and sudden heightened awareness of the reality of God's Holy presence. A hunger and desire to be fed by the Word of God is the natural inclination produced in the newly reborn individual and one of the key indicators that such an experience has truly occurred.

This articulation denotes the basic transformative process that any new creation in Christ will experience. No amount of personal will or belief in God can or ever will result in the miracle of the New Birth (John 1:12-13).

In Jesus' Missionary Discourse to His apostles, as recorded in Matthew 10, Jesus made a particular statement that many have struggled to understand:

"Think not that I have come to send peace on earth: I came not to send peace, but a sword. For I am come to set a man at variance against his father, and the daughter against her mother, and the daughter- in-law against her mother-in-law. A man's foes shall be they of his own household."

Matthew 10:34-36

While this statement was a bold and daring proclamation to those who heard these publicly spoken words, the timeless truth it confers maintains its relevance in the present reality of those who have passed from death to life in an authentic salvation experience. What was intended as an open renouncement from the ways of the law- entrenched majority amongst whom Jesus was commissioning the apostles, was also telling of another imminent reality new believers would soon come to understand.

I have witnessed first-hand what the upheaval of a family looks like when God saves one of its members. The unsaved of that household often despise the newly regenerated member because they are affected, to an extent, by the permeating Spirit of God's presence at work in and around that individual's life now present in the family home. This seemingly unwarranted conviction brought about by this operation of God upon those impacted is the cause of divisiveness and even deep-seeded resentment toward the one saved. Accusations of the newly regenerated putting on a "holier than thou" air are commonplace in these situations, although the individual could never be less guilty of such an act, being that he or she is living in the humblest possible state of their life because of what God has done inside them. They have been reborn; they are as harmless as a newborn baby and anyone who would hate a baby is the one with the problem.

The fact that unregenerate people can be affected by a spiritual transformation within someone else's life in their midst only validates the authenticity of such an experience. It is likely the reason for the tumult because the convicted are faced with a new intangible reality they cannot quite grasp nor refute. When light shines in the darkness, the darkness must and always will retreat.

Darkness is simply the absence of light, and because man is inherently sinful, even when he is exposed to the convicting light of God's presence afresh in someone else's life, he often becomes patently aware of the shame of sinfulness in his own and it renders him unnerved. It is the primary reason for division that occurs within the household of a newly saved person.

The need of man to be saved is universal and yet specific. However, man has an inborn tendency to merit God's gracious work of salvation, something that will earn him this undeserved grace just as the sorcerer Simon, in the Book of Acts chapter 8, thought that by offering money to the apostles, he could receive the gift of the Holy Spirit. This occasion uncovered the truth that the underlying motives of his belief and subsequent baptism were obviously impure because the Holy Spirit was not granted to him as it is granted to all those who have legitimately believed. Though the Holy Spirit at that time was administered only through the apostles, this incident underscores that he was never drawn by the Spirit to believe in the first place and, therefore, was not truly saved.

Simon's case lends credence to the fact that belief and baptism accomplish nothing apart from the initiating work of the Spirit. His inability to acquire the Spirit, based on this method, illustrates this point quite clearly. Though he was masquerading in a life of conversion, based on his alleged profession and the subsequent water baptism amongst the other believers, his cover was now blown, and the charade was over.

Collectively, churches today are filled with these kinds of conversions. They seem to have lost sight of the fact that it is the work of the Lord that initiates the salvation process. Instead, we have taken a full-blown, bull by-the-horns approach, pushed God aside, and led people through a "how to" formula, skipping over the most essential role in the process - God's calling. A Matthew 7:13 "wide gate" approach if ever there was one.

The recipients of Paul's letters, though many of them were brand new Christians, understood without question what the Church today seems to have forgotten. It was evidently clear to them that the miracle of the New Birth was not something obtained by works, asking, or choosing because it was never an issue that was addressed in any of his writings, and Paul addressed just about every problem one could imagine the Church having.

These churches witnessed, first-hand, the power of God working through the anointed gospel preaching of the apostles. There is no documented confusion on this subject recorded within the 21 New Testament epistles of the biblical canon, yet the unregenerate man's determination to, at some point, discover a formula to earn God's favor is an innate tendency inborn within him that knows no bounds. Perhaps, in his finite thinking, he considers that an effort to please, appease, or impress God will merit His approval and blessing. Most would never admit this, but the logic of man has often tried to find its way into the favor of God. I believe that Cain must have had such a thought. As his only brother at the time, I'm sure Cain could have attested to Abel's righteous character and likely attributed it to God's favor of him.

I believe Cain's attempt to earn God's approval is part of the reason his sacrifice was rejected, but what Cain was unable to realize was that the very work of his hands not only defiled his offering, but it apparently lacked the sacrificial element fit for an offering to God, and when he saw, in contrast, that Abel's offering pleased the Lord, it sparked the insidious jealousy that led him to murder his only brother.

In this account of Abel, we have an example of a perfect and undefiled offering. We have a lamb without blemish, the firstling and best of his flock, whose shed blood emulated the sacrifice God provided in the Garden of Eden when He made the coats of skins to cover the shame of Adam and Eve; a picture of the perfect future sacrifice God would require of Himself in the person of the Lord Jesus Christ- the Lamb of God slain from the foundation of the world and firstborn among many brethren who would serve as the ultimate sacrifice for the forgiveness of the sins of man.

Most believers fail to understand the spiritual language used in the Bible due to a lack of granted revelation. The language and ministry of the Gospel is literal and yet spiritual intending to produce a supernatural effect in the chosen. There is meaning within those pages that transcends the literal printed word and the realm of our natural understanding. It is the supernatural realm where faith comes by hearing and hearing the Word of God. It is the realm where the Spirit of God operates in the hearts of men. It is the language used by God to apprehend the soul through the men of God who facilitate the work of the Spirit, those who are sold out for Jesus and wholly surrendered to His will.

This is not to say that the Scriptures were intended to be spiritualized by men, but rather, the opposite holds true.

"It is the glory of God to conceal a thing: but the honour of kings is to search out a matter".

Proverbs 25:2

I've heard my fair share of pastors exclaim that your salvation experience doesn't necessarily have to be some epic occurrence and that you don't necessarily have to feel saved to be saved. This is more than doctrinal difference; this is a lie that has generated a tremendous amount of confusion amongst God's people. I can't imagine the number of souls that have been fed this nonsense by their spiritual leaders. It is highly unfortunate that we have men of God in pulpits all over the world who cannot articulate what authentic salvation is like. Unfortunately, I have never in my life heard a pastor say what I'm about to explain.

When a person encounters the all-consuming holy presence of God in their midst, and they realize their sinfulness in light of His perfect holy love, their world is turned right side up; the moment is epic and momentous. It's not to be compared to anything else in this life. The conviction of our sinfulness that the Spirit of God illumines in our heart brings us to our knees and forever changes us. The very fact that we acknowledge and experience the shame of our own sinfulness in an encounter before Him validates our granted saving faith and instantaneous repentance toward Him, and we realize as our heart reaches out for Him in total submission, that we are experiencing true surrender to His lordship in obedient reciprocity. Knowing our forgiveness has been made sure; we experience the genesis of our "new creation". You not only feel saved, but the euphoria you experience is so inexplicable that no one can convince you otherwise.

Your salvation has come! Everything you thought you ever knew about who God is, is set in order in an instant, and the quest to know Him more is forever set in motion. What you thought you understood holiness to be is ineffably defined in that moment, bearing an immeasurable depth of meaning you never saw coming, but now realize was grossly underestimated and could never have been anticipated or explained. Reverence for and holy fear of God is your new reality. It's as if someone finally turned on the light of your life, and that person is The Light of Life, the Lord Jesus Christ, whose made it possible for you to live eternally, forevermore in His presence, through this new existence. You have something that money cannot buy, and death cannot take away. The angels are rejoicing! You have been saved! You have been born-again!

A favorite old country preacher that I enjoy listening to now and again once used an analogy to describe what happens at the moment of salvation. I use it from time to time to explain this phenomenon that eludes so many believers. It goes something like this:

Let's say, for instance, that a bumble bee flew into the room and found its way into your shirt. Notice that there are three things that would take place: #1, The bumble bee would notify you of his presence; #2, There would be an immediate change in your behavior; and # 3, There would be lingering effects.

When the Holy Spirit of God opens the eyes of one's heart, an individual has an encounter with the God of the universe Himself, who has a way of making His presence crystal clear without saying a word. Secondly, there is such a devastatingly profound effect on the individual that their demeanor, tone of voice, and facial expression can hardly express what they are now feeling inside. Thirdly, the authenticity of this powerful event moves an individual to wholeheartedly pursue that of the Divine and the things that please Him. This includes a sudden deep interest in the Bible, Church and a compelling need to tell others what He has done in their life and serve Him in some capacity.

Unfortunately, many people's "salvation" experience sounds like mine once did as a young adolescent. Sure, no one could convince me otherwise that Jesus was the Son of God, that He died on the Cross for my sins, was buried and rose again on the third day, and ascended to the right hand of the Father. I knew these things to be so, at least on an philosophical level. I was convinced not only of the truth of these facts but also of the promise of eternal life that my church so insistently assured me of. What I realized, some 17 years later, was that my attempt to come to God, despite my most sincere efforts, was never the way He would intend. The most sobering truth I ever had to face was that the difference between what I had convinced myself of versus what God actually does in the salvation process has absolutely no place in the same discussion and is nowhere near the plane upon which He operates. I had a head-knowledge of Christianity in my heart, but what I lacked was the heart-knowledge in my soul that would, one day manifest and produce this forever-changed life. A transformation so unexpected and inexplicable that words have not yet even been imagined to ever possibly describe this glorious experience. Any question or doubt regarding my eternity was forever settled, once and for all, by the Amen, the Faithful and True Witness, The Beginning of the Creation of God, forevermore in my soul.

The reality I had to face was the contrast that the Lord would eventually make clear to me between what I once believed with all my heart and what I know today beyond all knowledge. In retrospect, I see how me confessing my sins and pouring out my heart in sincere repentance is not what procured my justification; my decision to believe in Jesus and trust in His finished work upon the cross is not what redeemed me; and neither was praying the sinner's prayer with tears falling fiercely from my eyes, begging God to save me, what made Him my Savior.

This profane deception is being sold every single day, and our churches have bought into and promoted this damnable teaching. Our sanctuaries, Sunday school classes, and information centers are polluted with Bible tracts and other paraphernalia that teach this lie from Hell. We have people in the name of God, thinking that they are doing Him service by handing these tracts out all over the world because they are incapable of effectively presenting a Savior they've never truly known. Steadfast, yet unaware they are assisting the Devil by sowing tares amongst the wheat in the garden of evangelism.

The Book of Romans contains a wealth of information on the subject of the believer's salvation, but unless one is a born-again believer, such as the intended recipients of Paul's letter to the Romans, it's entirely too easy to misconstrue many critical passages. For instance, a small section of Romans chapter 10 touches on the very subject at hand. While Paul is clearly sharing his burden for Israel's salvation and presenting his case of how the Gentile's election of grace was spurred by Israel's unfortunate rejection of their long-awaited Messiah, he makes the point that there is no distinction between the Jew and the Gentile concerning God's elective plan.

In making this distinction, Paul makes some statements that are easy to take at face value and can be very difficult to discern for the average reader. For example, Paul's allusion to Deuteronomy 30:11, 14 to make his point in verse 8, chapter 10 of Romans, that "...The word is nigh thee, even in thy mouth, and in thy heart: ..." indicating a revelatory truth that is evoked in the spoken word of God, actively present and very much alive, laying the basis for verse 9: "That if thou shalt confess with thy mouth the Lord Jesus, and shalt believe in thine heart that God hath raised him from the dead, thou shalt be saved."

The belief in our hearts spoken of in verse 9 is not simply a determination to believe. This approach is a complete misapprehension of the passage. The passage must also be read and understood in its entirety. We do not simply spew out some magic words and speak our New Birth into existence, as is the practice of so many. The passage itself is explained further in detail in the subsequent verses.

In verse 10, the "heart" that is used to believe unto righteousness is a newfound heart-knowledge of Jesus Christ granted solely by the mercy of God through His gracious granted faith (Romans 9:16). It is a revelation of His truth and existence evoked and initiated by the drawing power of God's Holy Spirit and subsequent conviction of our sin. The "confession" (v10) that is made unto salvation is not simply a profession, but an outward expression of an inward change (testimony) engineered completely by God. Therefore, in verse 11, "… whosoever believeth on him shall not be ashamed" attests to the fact that not only will the newly regenerated believer never regret his newfound faith, but his salvation will also never be contingent upon his ability to fulfill the demands of the Mosaic law (Romans 10:4).

In verse 12, Paul distinguishes God's revealed plan of salvation that is now inclusive of the Gentiles, then proceeds to declare (v13), "For whosoever shall call upon the name of the Lord shall be saved.". It is important to discern that this declaration does not indicate that a plea to God for salvation saves them. This idea couldn't be more contextually distorted. However, it is worth pointing out that those who can call on Him are merely reciprocating their acknowledgment of Christ's personal revelation to them. To "call" on Him is the soul's positive response to the inward drawing and conviction that God performs on an individual's life and is the very moment that the Savior also becomes his Lord.

The fact that God's salvation is no longer offered exclusively to the Jewish nation is also expressed. "How then shall they call on Him in whom they have not believed?" (v14) again, our calling out to God does not initiate the mode of salvation; it is a response to Him. More directly, it is a response to the drawing and conviction brought about by His Spirit. The belief that one must have in place is the revelation of His truth and existence, as previously stated. It is the spiritual confrontation of His presence and the convicting power of His holiness that initiates this response in the heart of the individual, not the intellectual assent.

Verse 14b,c "… and how shall they believe in Him in whom they have not heard?" These verses assert that God has chosen a principal means whereby one can be saved, and that is through the anointed preaching or declaration of a heralder. The exposure of an individual to the person and message of the Cross is the ordained method whereby the all-powerful presence of the Spirit of Christ is encountered (supporting the necessary work of personal revelation). While the heralder is responsible for disclosing these realities in his preaching to facilitate this work, the Holy Spirit is the principal force by which this truth is ultimately revealed.

Verse 15 declares that the man of God must be "sent" or *apostello* in the Greek meaning "set apart". This work is to be performed by a man who is called by the Lord, not a career pastor. While it is imperative to understand that God is never at the mercy of man's assistance to effect this regenerative work, this verse denotes the kind of man God qualifies to effectively herald the Gospel declaration.

After Paul's allusion to Isaiah's prophecy in verses 15 and 16, Paul concludes that faith comes by hearing God's Word (v17). God has chosen the foolishness of preaching (1 Corinthians 1:21) to save them that believe. Not those who believe to be saved, but those whom He saves will, thus, believe in the fullest sense of the word.

As it is critical to consider the context in any book of the Bible, one of the most important assessments to make when reading any of the New Testament epistles is the often overlooked and understated fact that the intended recipient of every single letter was addressed to a born-again audience. The early Church understood this and clearly had a better understanding of the Old Testament references Paul used, likely due to their greater familiarity with them, as the Old Testament was all the scripture that existed at that time. With these most pivotal pieces of information, the actual meaning of these somewhat obscure passages is brought into focus, with a level of detail and clarity that, admittedly, before, would have gone largely unrealized.

I hope you can now see that there is more to this passage than meets the eye: how its often overlooked and disregarded context changes its entire meaning and how this section of scripture was never intended to serve as a basis for formulating a path into the kingdom of God. That which, for so long, has been errantly endorsed and promoted by the Church has been done so at the expense of countless souls and to her own detriment.

Remember, the best lie is the one that sounds most like the truth. Satan knows this and when people are carelessly dealt with in this way, they are not only being misled by the people who claim to most want to help them, but those soliciting these perversions are assisting the enemy in his mission to thwart the primary ministry of the Church. Hence, the reason Paul's admonition to Timothy is so utterly imperative:

"**Study to shew thyself approved unto God, a workman that needeth not to be ashamed, rightly dividing the word of truth.**" 2 Timothy 2:15

For centuries, various defenders of the protestant faith have staked their claim in differing theological camps. Two main schools of thought have emerged dominant throughout the centuries and continue to be at the center of debate in many theological circles. They are doctrinal positions that emerged in the 16th century, and both coined after their respective founders: Arminianism after Jacobus Arminius, a Dutch reformed theologian, and Calvinism after John C. Calvin, a French reformed theologian.

Of these two schools of thought, in the matter of God's redemptive program for mankind, one of these positions emphasizes the volition of man, or his free will, while the other emphasizes the sovereign will of God. However, these two primary schools of thought may differ, they share an irony of commonality between them. Despite all of their theological efforts to distinguish themselves apart, their major pitfall lies in each camp's failure to articulate a descriptive comprehension of the salvific process, leaving this most marvelous mystery and its adherents in the dark, figuratively speaking.

While the element and character of God's sovereignty are realized by both camps, there are several points of contention between the two perspectives that are often the topics of heated debate.

A clear understanding of the positions that each group presents is vital for the avid Bible student to consider in developing his or her own perspective on these key theological positions. While this discourse assays to highlight the important premise of this debate, it is not intended to, in any way, serve as a formal treatise on the subject. The burden of comprehensive research to gain a fuller grasp of the positions held by each camp is incumbent upon each student's diligent motivation to acquire such. This will be most essential if the desire is to truly equip oneself to render an informed and insightful opinion. Of these two schools of thought, there are, of course, many points of contention in their respective positions.

The five tenets of traditional Calvinism include: Total Depravity, Unconditional Election, Limited Atonement, Irresistible Grace, and Perseverance of the Saints. However, at this time, of them, only one is most notably relevant to this discussion, the doctrine of Limited Atonement. Aside from Total Depravity, Limited Atonement is the principal tenet upon which all the other tenets hinge and is the primary sticking point that so divides these two parties. The argument being whether the atonement Christ provided on the cross was for the whole of mankind or for a specific few.

An exception to this, arguably, most defining tenet of the Calvinist's theology, would, no doubt, allow for the prospective existence of a universal salvation, as the Arminian camp has so presumptively insisted; however, the necessary breach would not only dismantle and undermine the entire framework upon which systematic theology affords the written Word of God to be academically understood, it would come at the expense of the supernatural intent of its message.

While recipients of this atonement consist of both Jew and Gentile alike, the sticking point for the Arminian camp lies in their inability to understand and accept a limitation upon that which they believe Christ proffered to the world.

Calvinists, who rely staunchly on context and a systematic approach to doctrine, point out that Christ was not sent to atone for the sins of the whole world on the hope that some *might* believe in Him and accept His finished work upon the cross but rather that He effectually laid down His life to specifically carry out the propitiation required of the Father to make atonement for the sins of those for whom God had determined in eternity past to elect.

The misapplication of biblical atonement applied by the Arminians to infer that Christ's blood atoned for the sins of the whole world is supported by verses such as Titus 2:11 which states:

> **"For the grace of God that bringeth salvation hath appeared to all men."**

While this scripture reference, which is only one of a few that is cited to defend the Arminian argument for an Unlimited Atonement, it becomes patently obvious that a consideration in favor of this position is most necessary to provide a basis upon which to support the framework of further unsubstantiated doctrine, namely the Arminian view of Conditional Election. Regardless of the fact that the Arminians' misconception concerning the foreknowledge of God, at this point, becomes immaterial, it is critical to note that Christ's atoning work will only apply to the total sum of God's elect in the end.

Because of the seemingly hardline position of the 5-point Calvinists, primarily regarding Limited Atonement, as it pertains to the salvation of the elect only, Arminians find themselves in adamant opposition due to their pursuit of evangelical aspirations in fulfillment of their belief in the Great Commission which brings to the surface another point of contention with Arminianism that infers Calvinists somehow assume relief from their evangelistic obligations, due to their belief that, in the end, only the elect ultimately will be saved. An attitude such as this would arguably warrant criticism, but there is no basis upon which to pin such an accusation against an entire faction.

The need of some within the Calvinist camp to disassociate themselves from the 5- point Calvinists arises as they find themselves in disunity on this concern and, at the same time, ill-equipped to defend their stance against the influential argument of their Arminian counterpart. As a result, a sect splintered from the 5- point camp in a seeming compromise from the most notorious position that has historically defined Calvinism. The contention spawned a more moderate brand of Calvinism known as Moderate or 4-point Calvinism.

However, a contradiction ensues within the 4-point camp in their continued struggle to reconcile their newfound misapplication of atonement with their continued insistence on an Unconditional Election. Problems tend to persist in even the most methodical approaches to a theological framework. When dogma finds itself at the mercy of assumption, uncertainty emerges, and clarity of context is left wanting.

Regarding the Calvinist doctrine as it pertains to their argument for a Limited Atonement, a failure to properly articulate an assessment of the encompassing totality of the elect, that is, all that are or ever will be, appears to be a non-existent component in their attempts to theologically assuage themselves from their detractors.

The "elect" are not the "elite". They are not preferred; they are not chosen because of their own merit or uniquely intrinsic values. They are the "whomsoever" our Lord will call, chosen in eternity past by Him who works all things after the counsel of His own will.

The truth is that man does not know the sum of the elect. Only God, by His omniscience, not His foreknowledge, does He know who will be saved, and God's omniscience is beyond the realm of our purview and, therefore, leaves us with only speculation, but the enlightened mind need only rely on the revealed character of God in scripture for understanding on this topic. Therefore, God's omniscience is also an indefensible argument for the Arminian view that God somehow "foreknew" from the beginning who would choose to "accept" Him based on their understanding of His foreknowledge. The Scriptures are quite clear concerning the sovereign election of God and that His redemption is premised solely upon the gracious act of His love for mankind irrespective of man's inability to choose Him (Romans 3:10- 12).

Though most Arminians typically lean on more of a "free grace" theology, the more traditional adherents often fall prey to the misapplication of perseverance teaching. Perhaps the idea of God's undeserved and bestowed grace, combined with man's inability to grasp the doctrine of Eternal Security, impresses a duty of obligation upon his guilty heart to pursue a path of works whereby the assumed appeasement and favor of God may be procured to insure his destiny.

Though adamantly refuted by its adherents, Arminianism, which has become the predominant view of both modern and postmodern Protestant Christianity, is a position that enmeshes its adherents in a works-based salvation. Evidenced by an emphasis on decisional-regeneration, a free will approach that imposes man's contribution of the presumed virtues of intrinsic faith and repentance to merit the approval and acceptance of God is, somehow, the self-generated substance that is allegedly responsible for the ignition of perpetual fire that only a supernatural transformation could ever spark. Further, their insistence on the promise of eternal life being conditioned upon such perseverance in a self-summoned faith is perpetually juxtaposed by the

Arminians' unmitigated failure to reconcile the context of passages regarding the doctrine of Eternal Security.

A slew of movements and denominations have been borne out of Arminian-based theology. The Holiness movement is one such example from whom select proponents believe that a life of perfect obedience and devoted servitude, known as sinless perfection or total sanctification, is attainable in this life while subject to the fleshly desires of our old sinful nature, and that acquisition of such is conditional upon his or her entrance into God's kingdom. The denial by a true child of God that his sinful nature still exists apart from his regenerated life is not only an unrealistic perception of one's self, it is a non-discerning approach to understanding truth.

A systematic approach and proper teaching of scripture clearly support the doctrine of Limited Atonement as well as predestination. While they may be difficult concepts for man to comprehend, they are a fundamental and integral aspect of God's redemptive plan as illustrated throughout the Old and New Testaments. They cannot be disregarded simply because they are difficult concepts to fathom, but a clear and balanced understanding of scripture recognizes that a God- designed plan of salvation is infinitely perfect and beyond the scope of man's ability to measure or judge. While the atonement will only apply to the sum of the elect in the end, we must also understand that God has not yet finished calling out His children.

The predestination of believers is based upon God's foreordained decree to provide salvation to mankind. Scripture has demonstrated over and again that God always sets apart a remnant. The fact that God has set apart a remnant in eternity past combined with the fact that He is also omniscient does not give us license to predicate that those of whom are known to be elect were so elected due to any quality God foresaw in them, nor does it permit us to conclude that those presently known to be elect are, in fact, the only ones that ever will assume this designation.

Throughout history, God has shown us a pattern in scripture of always sparing a remnant for His own sovereign purposes. The predestination of believers appears to signify such an allotment as the 144,000 souls of the Book of Revelation suggests. This very number used by God in describing the elect remnant souls of Israel is indicative of a unit of perfect totality beyond that of favor or preference. As God is no respecter of persons, the arrival at this conclusion is of reasonable estimation.

Either way, God has made it clear that He has a special program in place for the elect of the nation of Israel in the end times and has distinguished it apart from the program for the Bride of Christ, the elect who will be gloriously translated at the Rapture.

Mistakenly, many Bible passages are interpreted by believers to suggest that the emphasis of knowing Christ falls on the responsibility of man. However, it is the inherent spontaneous misstep of the natural mind to ascertain the interpretation of that which may only be known through revelation. The following scripture reference will be used to substantiate this point:

"Verily, verily, I say unto you, He that heareth my word, and believeth on Him that sent me, hath everlasting life, and shall not come into condemnation; but is passed from death unto life." **John 5:24**

In the above-cited passage, the meaning of the word "hearing" is obviously used in the figurative sense, intending to evoke a spiritual response as consistent with many such declarations made by Christ. One need only consider the context in which these words were spoken to quantify their meaning. When we "hear" by the Spirit of God, our understanding will be made fruitful by the operation of God. Our conversion is never consummated by our initiation. That is religion. Our faith is not founded on theory; it is made viable by the personal enlightenment of God's grace. Listening to and obeying the Spirit daily through the Word of God becomes the instinctive desire of the "new creation" and is how we are enabled to obey the Word of God in faithfulness.

It is imperative for man to understand that God's motivation for saving anyone is an immutable act of grace based purely on His great love for mankind. He provided a way to save us because only a perfect sacrifice would appease His wrath against sin. Scripture's clear implication that there will be those who will come to believe unto salvation and that there will be those who will not, speaks less of God's omniscience and more to a provision of divine elective planning implemented by a sovereign God. The judgment of sin is inevitable, and its punishment imminent. God is just and will not permit sin to reign forever. The fact that God has elected to choose a remnant of creation for His own good purpose and pleasure is solely a prerogative and an enactment of sovereignty all His own. A divine decree established in eternity past that is in no way influenced by the determining factors of all that exists, including the will of man.

There's no prayer or magic formula that brings about the New Birth, contrary to the ABC approach of many traditional Protestant churches who advise summing up the following in a "sinner's prayer":

A - Admit you are a sinner in need of a savior.
B - Believe in the finished work on the Cross by the Lord Jesus for your sins.
C - Confess your sins, repent, ask for and receive by faith God's forgiveness.

First of all, the gravity of one's sinful condition can never be fully realized apart from the encountered convicting presence of God's Holy Spirit. As such, people are inherently oblivious to the person and work of Jesus Christ, let alone knowing Him as Lord. Therefore, convincing anyone of their need for a savior, reaches beyond that of mere assent and admission on the part of the individual to accept that which he is clearly unable to discern for himself. God never requires our consent or assent to the facts of the Gospel to be saved. This would imply the unfounded notion that salvation is conditioned upon the acceptance of man.

Then there is the approach of: "Believe, Receive, Become" as made popular by a 2017 Hollywood production. Let me just say that the Bible doesn't teach us that we cross the bridge to God, but rather God bridges the great chasm by meeting us where we are, as illustrated in the Gospel account:

"Ye have not chosen me, but I have chosen you and ordained you, that ye should go and bring forth fruit, and that your fruit should remain: that whatsoever ye shall ask of the Father in my name, He may give it you."

John 15:16

We can admit, believe, confess, receive, and become until we are blue in the face. We may have ourselves and everyone else around us convinced, but God is not mocked. The facts are that you cannot effectually admit you are a sinner, accept Jesus Christ as Lord and Savior, believe that Jesus' finished work on the cross atoned for your sin, receive His forgiveness and gift of grace, or even confess your sins or His lordship over your life until He has personally perpetuated the sequence of these events by the transforming power of His encountered presence.

Noah, Abraham, Isaac, Jacob, and Moses along with the prophets and apostles of the Bible, all have one thing in common. Each of them had revelatory proof of the existence of God. It is through the testimony of these men that the Word of the Lord has been made known unto man. Each of these men's experiences, though unique, all bear the same hallmarks of the salvation equation. The Bible teaches that salvation is by grace through faith and is the consistent method God always uses. While this fact has and always will be contingent upon God's sovereign election, which speaks to the grace factor of salvation, each of these men received something the moment that the Word of the Lord came to them, and that something was the gracious granted gift of saving faith.

Pastors and teachers have employed the use of the word faith primarily to suggest that man has an inborn virtue that can somehow condition the results of God's decreed plan if it is sincere enough. I want you to see that the faith that saves us is a granted faith and is not found naturally in man nor in his ability to somehow conjure it or arrive at obtaining it on his own.

The documented auditory evidence that scripture provides of these men all having heard the voice of God in His instruction to them instilled within them an immediate driving force and call to action that is the result of this gift of saving faith.

Hearing the audible voice of God was, quite simply, God's revelation of Himself to them. Otherwise, how could they have ever known Him in an experiential way, believed Him, or reacted to His instruction? Called by His grace, their natural response immediately reflects the transmitted gift of saving faith that God's gracious revelation always provides. That response is the action of obedience.

While God may not have revealed Himself audibly or visibly to man since biblical times, God's personal revelation of Himself to individuals through His Holy Spirit is how lives are transformed and remains to be the mode of salvation of anyone who has a genuine testimony. It is how saving faith is granted. It is how God has always saved those elected to salvation, through revelation, making Himself known personally. This method has never changed. It is the way that God has purposed and demonstrated since the beginning. The Word of God is the revelation of Himself to man and whether written or spoken, when the Spirit of God is facilitating that revelation, the salvation of man is the result.

"All things are delivered unto me of my Father: and no man knoweth the Son, but

Matthew 11:27

An example of this necessary revelation appears in chapter 9 of the Gospel of John, where Jesus encountered a man who was born blind.

Based on the text, it is apparent that this blind man grew up in a religious family. His parents attended synagogue near the place where Jesus found him. After his miraculous encounter, the man, when speaking with the Pharisees, exhibited some knowledge of God, seemingly, a little more than some who claim to believe today. Though this man exhibited evidence of belief in God, perhaps, even after his unanswered prayers to receive his sight, if even only for a moment, no amount of wishing, hoping, or desiring to see again was going to produce it.

It's the same with the New Birth. No amount of wishing, hoping, or desiring can bring it about. The formula man has contrived over time from his literal translation of misconstructed Bible passages has birthed only delusion and deception, and this deception has been used by the Church to seduce masses of souls all over the world for generations in a futile attempt to fulfill the directive of the Great Commission.

The fact is, we are all born blind spiritually. Only the miraculous New Birth that God initiates in an individual's life can cause us to see the light. The only, and most powerful, testimony the man born blind had was:

$$\text{"... one thing I know, that whereas I was blind, now I see." John 9:25b}$$

The burden of proof does not rest upon the shoulders of the individual whose life was changed. The changed life is the evidence and living proof that speaks for itself and volumes over the arguments of any who would ever doubt.

John 5:36

The once blind man had likely always believed in God on a conscious level, but when Jesus restored the sight of his physical eyes and then confronted him, he immediately acknowledged Jesus as Lord and worshipped Him because the eyes of his soul were also now open.

You see, the miraculous workings of the Master in the Gospels are a picture of the same miraculous work that the risen Lord does in bringing an individual into eternal life. The born-again are the very product of God's supernatural work, whose testimony is ever substantiated by the transformational evidence of their witness.

Recognizing that salvation has never been about a choice that man must make, but is the exclusive external work that God performs upon the soul, should grant us resolve as the Church to more closely align ourselves with this facilitative operation of the Spirit, and serve as a caution to never again deviate from it in our preaching.

May our Lord's condemnation of religious leaders who fail to preach the way of salvation forever echo within the chambers of our conscience and being:

"But woe unto you, scribes and Pharisees, hypocrites! for ye shut up the kingdom of heaven against men: for ye neither go in yourselves, neither suffer ye them that are entering to go in."

Matthew 23:13

I would like to share a personal story with you about a time when men of God were still sensitive to the Spirit and understood that as a pastor or an elder of a church, there was a responsibility to recognize spiritual giftedness and the evidence of genuine transformation amongst the flock, and after carefully arriving at such a determination, conscious, intentional efforts were applied to mentoring and discipling said believers into maturing Christian witnesses. I received such an experience at Hillcrest Park Baptist Church in Arlington, Texas.

Hillcrest was my first home. It is the church I belonged to immediately following my salvation experience.

When I say that I "belonged" to this church, I'm not simply suggesting that I was just a member there. I'm saying that I was welcomed, as family, with arms wide open, by the people of God.

The love of Christ was truly present in this precious body of believers, and the power and presence of God was at work within the fellowship of this dear assembly. I was a stranger, made to feel like a reunited loved one.

It all began with the interim pastor of that church, who was actually the church's administrator. This man, by the way, was doing an extraordinary job of standing in the gap while the congregation found itself in one of the most vulnerable situations a church could be in. They had been without a pastor, but by no means were they without a shepherd in the pulpit. It was this brother in Christ whose great discernment and sensitivity to the Spirit of God that gave direction and sound guidance to this "beacon of hope" in Arlington, Texas.

I remember walking from my apartment a few blocks away to Hillcrest the very first Sunday after my transformation. A man who was dead and on his way to Hell just hours before was about to enter the local church for the first time in his new life.

The place was packed except for one or two pews in the back near the foyer entrance, so I took the closest seat to the door so as not to disrupt the service. I don't remember making it in time for the music portion of the worship service, so I may have been a little late. I do, however, remember that the pastor made adequate eye contact several times from across the room during the message.

After the closing prayer at the end of service, I was the first one at the door, aside from the pastor, who was there to greet everyone as they exited. While shaking his hand and introducing myself, he looked at me very peculiarly as if he sensed something about me. It was as if, somehow, God caused him to take special notice of me outside of the fact that I was a new visitor. I smiled and gladly assured him that I would return again.

It was a blessed time for me. As I walked home, I remember feeling so special. I knew that God was with me and that He was guiding my first steps as a new creation in Christ. I remember telling Trula, my then-girlfriend, about the experience, and right away, we became involved with Hillcrest.

A couple of days later, one afternoon, this pastor came alone to visit us at our apartment. I later discovered that the church's visitation schedule usually consisted of two or more selected members from the visitation group and that visitations were typically made in the evenings. Anyway, I was able to share my testimony with him and my conviction to get married right away.

A couple of Saturdays later, Trula and I were married by this pastor in the sanctuary, courtesy of Hillcrest Park Baptist Church. Dozens of members who were total strangers to us threw us an extravagant and unbelievable wedding shower the next day after the service. Though the Church knew that we had previously been living together out of wedlock, with a child no less, we were never once made to feel like we were being judged. We were overwhelmed with the showering of gifts, especially the gift of this Church's unwarranted love and acceptance. It was a beautiful thing and a true picture of the unconditional love of Christ exhibited in an authentic, precious Church body.

Sunday, the very next day after we were married, my new wife and I came forward at the end of the service to join the Church. I believe that God used my testimony to move the heart of this man, and I know that he experienced the presence of God in a powerful way when he visited our home that day because the Spirit of God filled and rested in that apartment like a mist. When God found me, I immediately followed His instruction to spiritually "cleanse" my home by ridding it of any and everything we owned that did not honor, glorify, or please Him beginning that very moment. He, in essence, commanded me to make my house a house of prayer, and when I did this, the Spirit of the Lord, in effect, consecrated the atmosphere of our humble abode. I can't explain it. I don't expect anyone to understand it. It just was, and that's all there is to it.

This pastor, after we had come forward at the end of the service, introduced us before the Church and shared with the congregation a little bit about us and his visit to our home, and after a not so-awkward moment of silence, he gave a very loud and powerful declaration: "THESE TWO ARE ON FIRE!!! FOR JESUS!!!" and a roar came from the assembly who were moved out of their seats for the glory of God and the room was filled with praise for the works He had done. Let me remind you, this was a Southern Baptist Church. Trula and I were overwhelmed with the reception we received from the acknowledgment of the Lord to the people, and my heart was filled with wondrous joy for the God who is worthy to be praised.

I'm not saying that church membership experiences should necessarily look like ours did at this church because it certainly never happened like that again at any other assembly we had joined in subsequent years. However, I am saying that truly born-again pastors who are intimately walking with and pursuing the Lord, sensitive to His Spirit, passionately leading His people while joyfully doing His work, will not only experience the guidance of God's voice in their own lives but can experience it through the supernatural work He still does in our midst, and share in the blessing and joy of seeing the fruits of their labor in the lives of those God places within their paths.

This church was certainly attuned to the Spirit of God, and they, with great expectancy, were ready to experience Him as their hearts had been tenderly plowed in previous weeks by the diligent faithfulness of this Spirit-filled man of God.

The Lord knows that this warm and loving reception would probably not happen again until I go home to be with Him, but God let me experience it, not to give me cause to gloat, but rather to allow me to understand the joy of my salvation and of the angels in Heaven who rejoice over even one sinner who repents.

Now looking back, I realize that many were sensitive to the Lord's presence in and around me at that time. I suppose it was like the scent of a newborn baby to those great men and women of God that so attracted them. The presence of the Lord's fragrance, indeed, seemed to clothe my person and the air around me, and I believe that God was using this experience of my transformation as a reminder to those beloved saints that the work that the Lord does is not of this world, but of a supernatural element and living testament to the purpose for which we are so commissioned.

This experience left something in me that can never allow me to be content with going through the motions of formalistic religion. While the Christian life definitely has its fair share of highs and lows, a hope that has been given me from above drives my inner passion for experiencing a Christianity that is alive and burning fiercely in my heart.

Rise of the Unregenerate

"Man, motivated by his fleshly desires, once again imposes his preferences upon that which was divinely commissioned, and after all this time, his natural inclination still remains to carve the image of the god he envisions to serve."

People have associated going to church with right living as far back as any of us can remember. While this custom is certainly becoming an antiquated tradition, its motivation to continue has been largely spawned out of a sense of obligation to carry out the dutiful appeasement of our progenitors to somehow satisfy the minimal expectations of a guilt-imposing God, rather than a quest to truly know Him or further the work of His kingdom.

Since the September 11, 2001, attacks on the World Trade Center in New York, a wave of patriotism seemed to rise from a dormant sea of preoccupied Americans. A nation whose world was rocked and overcome with confusion and uncertainty found themselves vulnerable for the first time in decades against a false sense of security that has blanketed, so warmly, the freedoms that everyday Americans take for granted.

For so many, especially those who were directly impacted by this unfortunate event, this truly was a wake-up call. Many Americans, for the first time, found their patriotic spirit. Many, for the first time in a long time, found themselves looking to the Word of God for answers and assurance that all would be well again in their world.

Though God often uses suffering, sorrow, and the terror of sudden tragedy to get our attention, it would not be a fair assessment to assume that these attacks were ordered by God as a means of administering punishment upon America for its gross sin, as some have dared to suggest. Otherwise, where were the whole of God's retribution America is due for the abominable acts she has so flagrantly and unrepentantly committed for generations? Nevertheless, the fact remains that God does have a way of profoundly affecting us when calamities strike.

My heart goes out to all of those who were impacted by this event, and I commend those who, so bravely and without hesitation or regard for their own safety, responded to this devastating crisis. To those who experienced a genuine turning back to God as a result of this unfortunate tragedy, may God be ever magnified.

However, there was another wave that swept over America along with its newfound patriotism. This was a wave of religious revival, and many of those affected, motivated by fear and confusion from these acts of terror, found themselves returning to their religious roots.

Thank God for those who may have been truly saved through this tragedy. Unfortunately, a vast majority of these people did what many of us have done, especially as children; energized afresh with spiritual adrenaline, fleeting promises were made to God when it suited our needs. Promises that, in reality, we knew we could never live up to. These are those who want God's protection, favor, blessing, and provision but not necessarily His consistent involvement in their personal lives.

This particular group are those who've found their religion and patriotism at the same time and, in fact, have difficulty disassociating the two, especially when their true colors bleed through and the order of their priorities are exposed. Their sore displeasure with the hot political climate, as well as their utter disdain for the job our nation's leadership is doing, all take center stage in their heart and attitude and are reflected in their typical demeanor. You know the type. They're Americans first and believers after the fact. Full of conviction when it comes to political fallout and democratic injustice but lacking any real substance as a believer when it comes to spiritual candor or conviction. With their allegiances reversed, their emotions worn ever on their sleeve, and their opinions ever-present on their lips, the contamination of any alleged testimony they may have actually claimed is readily compromised at the expense of making their feelings known.

Having discovered, as of late, their patriotic spirit, many of these suddenly somehow reckon themselves an authority on biblical Christianity. Who knew that to be a Christian, all you had to do is love the Red, White, and Blue? Don't get me wrong, I love this country as much as anyone and enjoy the freedoms that our brothers and sisters have fought so courageously for. I will admit that I tend to agree with much of what is eating these people, but this is about where our true allegiances lie as God's people and our ability to represent the One who has given us self- control through the Spirit of grace.

I never cease to be amazed at just how "religious" people become when their world is affected by tragedy. We're all guilty of it at one time or another, but the faith that so many unlikely people suddenly proclaim in the face of disaster and sorrow is unprecedented. Where are these people in the day-to-day example of living when everything is right in their world? If these instances are truly legitimate acts of contrite hearts, may the charade be finally dropped, and these times of affliction and brokenness bring them back into the life that Christ has given them or perhaps, a work has begun in them that will, one day, produce the transformation that Heaven requires.

Despite our best efforts and intentions, we are mostly oblivious to and out of sync with when and how the Spirit of God is working in our midst. Our tendency to cluelessly and constantly get in the way of what God is doing is so often the cause of missed opportunity that we might otherwise be appointed to. So many of us have simply not realized this truth, and because of it, we continue to fall short in fulfilling our ministerial potential for seeing others genuinely saved.

May we, as God's people, learn humility and sensitivity to the work of the Spirit in our midst as well as the opportunities He presents for us to rise to the call of our God-commissioned objective.

Across the globe, evangelical churches are disappearing from the fabric of our society. Without question, the root cause of this phenomenon can certainly be attributed to the Church's ongoing systemic failure to clearly and faithfully present the Lord Jesus.

Where are the days of passionate John the Baptist-style preaching; where the Gospel was being declared in the power of the Holy Spirit and people were still experiencing authentic transformation within the Church? At what point did man arrive at the consensus that a decision for Christ would suffice and supersede the sovereign will and authority of God's almighty Word?

The Church used to be the voice of truth, reason, and morality in our culture, but now seems to be running for cover judging by the apologetic stance she has taken on her previous hardline convictions and dogmas. The compromise to subject herself to the placation of politically correct standards with a godless and Christ-hating society is an outrage and a shameful exhibition of tolerance to a fault. In her effort to become more socially acceptable, the Church has subverted herself by watering down her teachings and lowering her qualification standards for leaders as well as members. Christian, this ought not to be so.

For generations now, congregants have allowed their opinions and personal inclinations, biblically sound or not, to influence the Church's priority of reaching the lost. Man, motivated by his fleshly desires, once again imposes his preferences upon that which was divinely commissioned, and after all this time, his natural inclination still remains to carve the image of the god he envisions to serve.

This is further illustrated by the Church's ever-diminishing criteria for electing pastors and deacons. Under the presumption that preference has simply taken precedence, the practice of biblically vetting these important roles in the Church seems to have been rendered invalid by a complete and total lack of concern. It is more preferable to assign someone who appeals to the membership's personality rather than appoint someone who actually meets the scriptural qualification. Matters as crucial as this ought not to be left to the whims of the superficial.

We have reduced our standards in assessing whether a prospective pastor feels like a good fit for the assembly without regard to the Church's actual need for a divinely appointed shepherd. This speaks volumes regarding a congregation's depth of sincerity, whose priority for substance and purpose willingly takes a back seat to accommodate the preferential inclinations of the shallow.

Favoring style over substance and performance over participation, congregants of these establishments merely long to be satisfied with an adaptation of the worship that rightly belongs to God. Preferring imitation over an encounter, they are awed by the emotion of an impersonating presence of the Spirit. Their adoration of the golden calf they have fashioned has finally found center stage at the worship altar of God and is the spectacle upon which their praise has been found to be worthy.

The expectation of churchgoers to be moved and charmed by the heart-warming, ear-tickling messages that accompany these services is noticeably void of the Gospel truth and completely absent of the Holy Spirit, leaving personal accountability to sin at the door and the power of God to see people genuinely saved out of mind and sight. This is the product of unregenerate man's subtle rise and gradual overthrow of the tabernacle of God.

Local churches today consist of so few regenerated believers, if any, that the Church has not only lost her way, but she has also capitulated to the theft of her own identity, and in terms of her reputation, the fraudulent activity upon which her name this detriment has befallen begs the question if her recovery is beyond the hope of salvage.

Counterfeit churches have become the norm for today's religious society, and the vexed few elect who, over the years, have so stoically managed to endure through the ultra- progressive shift, apparently acclimated themselves long ago to the idea of a hopeless and gradual surrender.

The truth that some things simply must change over time is a reality whose acceptance must be faced, but when an endorsement from a former church, statement of faith, or willingness to be baptized carries more weight in granting one membership into a "house of God" than the obvious presence of the Holy Spirit in one's life or an actual testimony of salvation, it becomes abundantly clear that the focus and intent of these groups have little to do with the souls of man, and everything to do with the Almighty Dollar.

The trend of so many churches to cater and appeal to their audiences has become painstakingly obvious in their attempts to dazzle churchgoers with "worship facilities" that look more like television studios or upscale concert venues than a place where the peculiar and non-worldly people of God would ever dare imagine assembling this side of Heaven.

Man, in his unregenerate state, leaning to his own understanding, which is the principal mode of reasoning amongst the unsaved, devises a design of worldly appeal to accommodate the superficiality of specific classes of demography. The extremes to which he will go to develop an atmosphere of what he imagines will suit the persuasions of the affluent and prosperous are evident. The consideration that his congregant's inclination to invite others will be enhanced by providing a place with such an impressive allure has no doubt crossed his mind. It is, after all, the intention of this glamorous aesthetic to complement the crowning touch of the induced euphoric worship experience he purposes to evoke within its walls.

The brand of ultra-contemporary Christianity behind this movement has become the ideal standard of what a relevant church, in this day and age, should look like. However, this idea is so far removed from the Jesus who gave His life for the sins of His people that even anti-Christians seem less and less offended by the type of "believers" being produced by these outfits. Their faith may be non- denominational, but it's also non-confrontational, non- dimensional, a friend of the world, and an enemy of Christ.

This natural progression of man, attempting to discern that which can only be disclosed through revelation, has merely set a precedent for making up the rules as he goes.

Like curious children who've unearthed a mysterious board game from a forgotten chest, whose rules far exceed their patience and skill level; yet, intrigued by nostalgia and the thrill of adventure that surely awaits them, the children determined to unbox this newfound gem, proceed to play the game however they might imagine.

Left to their own devices and with total disregard for the rules or objective, they immerse themselves in blind delight, pretending to know how the game is played, making up the rules as they go, taking their turns at rolling the dice to discover the outcomes of their fortunes. Then, one day, when these children grow old and pass on the legacy of the charming labyrinth they've made of it, their children's children adopt the cursed heritage and carry on in the traditions and rules their predecessors so arbitrarily instituted.

To know the number of believers who approach the Bible in this way, would be beyond the realm of comprehension for some. However, due to the Church-at-large's ritual practice of unvetted tradition as well as the myriads of denominations, false doctrines, and cults present in our religious society today, the stark reality of this phenomenon is not only evident but is overtly impossible to deny.

The enemy has been sowing the seeds of his counterfeit Gospel for generations. When will the true men of God finally prioritize their purpose above their pride and prestige to do what is right, even if it means risking it all? How long will the Church permit the careless dealings with the souls of man to affect the prospective futures of the unsaved and allow the incessant defamation of our Savior's blessed name to continue?

A topic that will most assuredly expose the corruption within the typical local church is the subject of tithing. Try challenging the subject or practice of tithing, and you will see the horns of Satan come out of the same man they call the Senior Pastor.

Anyone who has ever objectively studied the practice of tithing now knows that churches are guilty of having abused its biblical context to extort financial support from godly yet uninformed and well-intentioned people for generations. Over time, the Church has turned into a "not-for- profit" business by man's corrupt teaching of the Word of God. Tithing was a command in the Old Testament during the dispensation of Law. In our present dispensation of Grace beyond the finished work of Christ upon Calvary, there is not found any mention of such a practice in the New Testament for the Bride of Christ.

It is regrettably shameful that church leaders, for centuries, have taken great advantage of the common man's ignorance of God's Word and used it to gain spiritual, emotional, and financial control over him. In fact, the emphasis placed on the education of pastors, as a major criterion for appointment consideration, often above any record of legitimate testimony, character, or reputation is not only unfortunate, but also seems to coincide with a very familiar secular strategy. It's no secret that in order to maintain their independence, these organizations rely solely on the constant petitioning of financial support from their members. Thus, the necessity for a dissimulated and mutually beneficial arrangement is fast realized whereby the administrative body must engage in a reciprocal relationship with the pastor whose purported trustworthiness and scriptural proficiency is consequently conditioned upon the church's endowment of imbued and reinforced validation, signaling to the congregation that the holder of the seminary degree is, indeed, the expert authority on biblical discernment and interpretation, so long as the funds continue to flow in.

People are often intimidated and feel inferior to those who are allegedly more knowledgeable on a particular subject, especially those of the biblical persuasion. Religious leaders know this and often use this leverage to sway those under their control and influence. I mean how many people are going to argue with a neurologist about any of the sciences of his specialized profession? Out of ignorance, the "sheep" cower with inferiority to any authority whose name is preceded by an honorific prefix.

Tithing, quite simply, is an Old Testament ordinance imposed upon a New Testament Church. The last time it is mentioned in the Bible is in Malachi, the last book of the Old Testament. It was addressed to an Old Covenant people but referenced often by church leaders today and relentlessly imposed upon the uninstructed and naive. Such conduct aches for the lash of the whip and begs the condemnation of Him whose temple we have so defiled.

For over 400 years, during the intertestamental period, it would have been customary to continue in the teachings and practices God had previously instituted. Though He was silent regarding any new revelation to man during this period, a new dispensation was about to begin. Obviously, the New Testament encourages generous living and giving, but it's the result of a life transformed by grace whose outward expression of a changed heart fuels this willingness to give.

Irrespective of the fact that the Church's sight, in this current Age, has grown dim and has all but given up on her primary objective of winning souls to the kingdom, spiritual leaders have certainly not relented in their pursuit to enforce the command of this non-contextual practice against God's people. Surely there are pastors who know the truth on this subject but do not possess the courage to ever speak with authority against the abuses of its long-standing tradition. Rather than take an unpopular stand on the truth, maintaining job security takes precedence at the flock's expense.

Most any pastor or leader on the church's payroll would be immediately dismissed and demonized for endorsing such an opposing position. Its exposure would literally embarrass and destroy the integrity of thousands of pastors and religious institutions likely sparking a mass exodus of disenfranchised believers. It's one of many considerations a pastor should contemplate prior to accepting a role within an organization that places a high emphasis on his obligation and responsibility to petition tithes.

My prayer is that one of these days, the real men of God will stand up and suffer that persecution head-on and bring back to the Church what's been lost. However, the truth is not marketable. People do not fill up stadium-size parking lots to hear the truth. The truth often hurts and is very divisive (Hebrews 4:12). Jesus knew this better than anyone. Especially aware of the motives of the majority of the multitudes that followed Him, He knew what was in man, and refused to place confidence in him (John 2:25).

Let me remind you that the local church is not who Jesus is coming back for, so make sure your motives are pure and never based on what others expect or will think of you.

In the Church's move to adopt and institute tithing as a biblical directive, she has defected from sound teaching and has turned the practice of cheerful giving into a "balance due for services rendered" situation. This is symptomatic of an institution that failed long ago to operate as it was originally intended, and now, to mitigate its failure to do it God's way, because he cannot, unregenerate man constructs his own means of procuring the financial stability required to continue the charade of playing Church.

Several years ago, after a bit of a sabbatical, my wife and I had returned to the fellowship of our then-home church in League City, Texas. One night, shortly after our return, we found ourselves attending a quarterly finance committee meeting where such items are discussed as the monthly budget, staff needs and expenses, missions and the like. The messages we were hearing in the weeks leading up to this meeting were quite sharp concerning the Church's disobedience to God in her giving.

We were not privy to anything concerning the Church's budget in our absence, but apparently, the leadership, including the Senior Pastor and the Associate Pastor, felt compelled to badger the membership and accuse them of being in rebellion against God because they were suddenly finding themselves in dire financial straits.

During this meeting, I couldn't help but feel sorry for the committed members of this church who were clearly being targeted. I felt like these pastors were beating us all over the head with this hapless and unwarranted accusation. After all, we were talking about the same crowd who were there every time the doors were open; the same crowd who regularly volunteered to work the nursery, serve in the kitchen, taught Sunday School, VBS and had obviously committed themselves financially long ago to the support of the Church's needs.

When the financial reports were passed around at the meeting, it had become clear what had been happening. Having been active members for a while, my wife and I knew what the staff salaries were previously.

We also experienced firsthand that any time the leadership wanted something that presented a challenge to the budget, they would play on the Church's kindheartedness and generosity and would pitch their proposal for needed funds with a steaming-hot potluck side dish of guilt. The Church loved and trusted the pastor and leadership staff wholeheartedly and worked however they could to support them in any way.

Evidently, in our absence, the flock was coerced into some outlandish salary increases. The leadership had convinced the finance committee and the rest of the assembly to vote in favor of making the Youth Pastor, the Children's Director, the Minister of Music, the Associate Pastor, and the Senior Pastor's jobs full-time salaried positions. I'm sure this didn't all happen in one meeting, but it happened just the same. Everyone's salary had doubled within one year's time, except for the Senior Pastor, whose income had increased to over four times what it had been a year prior, not-to-mention, he was now receiving full health benefits, a 401K and a retirement pension.

I'm not saying that this pastor wasn't putting in the effort because it appeared that he was sincerely devoted, but what perplexed me the most is the math that was used to determine the Church's budget. It was flawed from the outset because it was engineered to reflect an average dollar amount that committed members were giving times the number of people on the church's roll. It was also very clear that there were never as many people at these meetings, or even on Sunday morning, as the role suggested, not even close.

Only about a one-third of the people on the role were committed members, but because of an influx of membership earlier in the year, a budget was apparently formulated on that premise and unduly presented, pressured, and sold to the congregation and finance committee by the leadership who endorsed the plan, and it ended up splitting the Church, forced the layoffs of practically the entire leadership team and nearly closed the doors. Only the Senior Pastor and Associate Pastor remained. A short time later, the Associate Pastor was excused after his faithful assistance in brutally badgering the core membership's reputation and integrity to a pulp. Needless to say, the reunion was over and the time for my family's departure was at hand.

It's funny sometimes how God uses these experiences to teach us certain lessons. It's interesting that the Church knew it had been losing money all year, but now they clued into the fact that there was no way they would be able to sustain through the next year on their given financial trajectory, yet the mention of temporary sacrificial pay cuts never once entered into the conversation as an option to salvage the Church's mission of continuing the cause of Christ.

When a person is truly born-again, there is nothing that the new believer wants to do more than to please God. This is how I felt then and still feel today. Though He always supplied for my needs, God had allowed me to endure years of financial hardship even in the face of pure devotion. I believe that God was teaching me a valuable lesson, one that I would eventually come to learn and understand. Years would go by before I would eventually grasp the truth behind the Church's motivation for teaching it though.

The Church had bound tithing to lordship, and the two became inseparable for me. One of the most admired and respected preachers I'd ever heard made this connection early on in my Christian walk, and I was left in its trap for years.

One of the main reasons I believe God allowed me to struggle financially all that time was to help me learn the high cost of relying on the logic and understanding of others once and for all, and to instill in me a persistent discontentment that would fuel my quest for the hope of victory that could only be found in the Word of truth.

For years, I struggled to learn this lesson because in hindsight I realized, that despite my zeal to please God, I had been trapped in a years-long season of spiritual pride that blinded me from seeing the revelatory truth of this great plight. A vexation for which the Church-at-large has yet to express an ounce of recourse.

I understand that what I am saying must sound like total heresy to many of you who may not have yet discovered this liberating fact. I used to think the same way. However, a universal truth has taught me that sometimes a break from the circle you've surrounded yourself with helps you to gain a focus and perspective that you would otherwise be prevented from seeing because of how close you were.

I have learned that the journey of our faith continues on both sides of the fence. A truly born-again Christian who wrestles for truth despite his or her own blindness to certain realities can still learn something about the world, Christianity, and themselves, inside and outside of church fellowship. Our faith was never intended to exist solely within the confines of the church's walls. It is a journey that never truly ends as long as we live and breathe this side of Heaven.

The churches that God is really doing a work in do not obligate people to give; they advocate the passionate preaching of the Word of God, which results in people coming to the Cross under the convicting power of the Holy Spirit. In turn, people who are genuinely saved naturally want to live for God and when coupled with proper guidance for Christian living, are encouraged and motivated to live a generous life that pleases Him.

When this happens, regenerated people's natural response is to support the work of the ministry whether anyone passes a plate in front of them or not. When people are genuinely saved, the most natural thing they want to do is please the Lord and a little bit of right teaching on generous living and giving can go a long way to supporting the actual work of the kingdom.

True Churches are not built on the coerced pledges of man. They are not built on man's obligation to give under imposed conviction, nor are they built on money given with impure motives or out of what people think God expects of them. Newsflash! God has never needed our demon-possessed money for anything in the first place!

When people give under false pretenses and impure motives, they are merely contributing to building their very own Tower of Babel. Many congregants think that their monetary giving is a spiritual gift because they've been told it is by their short- sighted spiritual leaders who can't tell the difference between regenerated and religious. They tend to deem the lazy, inactive and often absent members as possessors of this "spiritual gift" because it's the only thing these can effectively contribute in terms of pulling the proverbial wagon up the hill. While it makes better business sense for these leaders to be inclusive rather than risk losing a member who's at least capable and willing to contribute financially, I must impart that one cannot even possess a spiritual gift without a testimony. The only spiritual gifts people without a testimony should be concerned with are the gifts of Grace, Faith, Forgiveness, Repentance, and Salvation. For without confirmation of having received these solely Spirit-granted gifts, all other such endowments remain inapplicable.

Generations of people have been brought up in the tradition of giving to hold a good seat in the local church, and pride themselves in taking ownership and credit for its establishment and ongoing success. These contributions, somehow, delude them into thinking that they are actually doing God's work, but they are only deceived by the false sense of security it buys them.

The typical 8% - 15% of monies that go to missions are largely the Church's dues for belonging to a mission board and often an excuse to exempt themselves from doing the evangelical work they claim they've been called to do. This is playing Church at its heart. Giving that money somehow eases the conscience of the lazy "believer" and often takes the spotlight off his spiritual disassociation.

Someone has once pointed out that if the missions that churches supported were successful, the need to financially support them would eventually cease. Outreach efforts ought to have reached some level of independence after a certain period. If the Church's missionaries are truly called and doing the work of an evangelist by faithfully presenting the Lord Jesus, their ministries should flourish with any reasonable determination. If they are not producing fruit, uproot and reassign them elsewhere. If, after an earnest period of effort, they persistently fail to produce, perhaps it is time to prayerfully consider what other avenues God may be working in. The work of God's kingdom is much too precious to waste on fruitlessness and procrastination.

When the Church fails to realize that her kingdom efforts and budget are being poorly implemented, squandered, or exploited, discerning believers must heed the Spirit's direction, resist the pressures of tradition and conformity, and, in faithful obedience, contend for the stewardship of her God-given resources. Today is the day for God's true children to open their eyes and take stock of what they have and are collectively buying into, fiscally and otherwise.

The reality that God is still saving the lost people of this world goes without saying, and because of this, the work of drawing the lost to Himself is ongoing, yet they are being turned away in droves by the negligent bias of the misguided and apathetic traditionalists. What was once a hospital for sinners has become a luxury resort for those masquerading as saints.

Many are those in whom God has begun a work that are often the inadvertent targets of harsh judgment and criticism by the very people who claim to represent the Lord Jesus. I have witnessed more than my fair share of spiritual leaders who viciously assault the integrity and motive of the entirety of the seeker-sensitive collective. Consequently, the seekers who are merely searching for answers, where they presumably ought to be found, are deemed guilty by association and share, in large part, the brunt of this unwarranted criticism.

The seeker-sensitive pastors appear to be the envy of many of these intolerable, envious, lazy, and hypocritical leaders of traditional churches who have infected, with great prejudice, their own congregants and turned them out of the way from the very work the Church was commissioned to do in the first place. As such, the lost sinner, depraved by his condition, yet in search of truth, carries on and subjects himself to another hopefully less cruel experience at the next house of God.

It's time that the Church realizes that the reason the world is not turned on to Jesus is because they've seen the famine that is the fruitless existence of our ineffective witness, whose testimonies lack transformation and are tainted by a powerless and unbiblical Gospel presentation.

By now, most of us should realize that seeing people truly saved takes more than simply just inviting them to church. Someone has to be that bold witness of Jesus. If not you, then who? More often than we'd like to admit, most of us have probably found ourselves disappointed, on more than one occasion, by the expectations we place upon the pastor to impact those, for Christ, whom we've invited to church.

We tend to place high expectations on the pastor to deliver a compelling message for others so that we do not have to do it ourselves. We, then, are left disappointed and disillusioned by a misunderstood and unfulfilled commission to reach the lost when the message your guest receives falls on deaf ears because it is completely inconsequential to their circumstances or eternal future.

When broken people visit a church's fellowship that leaves them with the same despair they walked in the front door with, though they may initially feel better about themselves for the effort made, they will soon withdraw at the conclusion that, perhaps, our God wasn't the answer they had hoped to find.

Lost people don't need Bible exposition, a lecture, or another lesson in futility by missing the whole point of their visit. Enduring messages of ranting and complaining about the partisan issues of a divided secular world is a complete waste of everyone's time. The pulpit is not a political platform for mud-slinging, nor is it a stage for talent shows or auditions for stand-up comic preachers to host a laughing revival.

What is the Church all about if God's people aren't truly about their Father's business? Church members will never be ordinately affectioned to consistently invite people to a service where an anointed passionate plea for the person of Christ is not being faithfully presented, but rest assured, that when God is truly working in the Church's midst, there will be no lack of motivation to invite others.

The service that your guest attends gives them a fairly clear picture of the God you worship. However, no one can testify of the God you serve better than you. If your church falls short in adequately presenting God to the extent He has impacted your life, then perhaps it's high time you get busy doing the work of evangelism yourself. Are you or are you not the elect of God? Do you not possess a testimony of salvation? Then save yourself the disappointment you set yourself up for by presuming that responsibility belongs solely to your pastor. Take ownership and use your God-ordained right to discerningly exercise that authority.

I understand that broken and hurting people are looking for answers, and they're going to eventually search for those answers where they think they ought to be able to find them. If that happens to be the local church, then let's not settle for being associated with the hypocritical, self-righteous, loveless, and Christ-less church that the watching world has already rejected. People have long since been turned off to Jesus by the fake, hypocritical majority who consistently and incessantly misrepresent Him.

People need to hear the Gospel presented in the power of the Holy Spirit, not another ineffective message downloaded at the last minute by some out-of-touch career pastor who's more concerned about his image and social profile than the very souls in his charge desperately in need of God to speak through him and breathe upon them the power of everlasting life. Thus, the indifference of those who would embrace such denial must realize that it comes not only at the expense of losing the race, but at the ultimate compromise of one's honor, purpose and identity.

Nowadays, to suppose that God is still going to speak through a donkey, a dead one at that, is beyond presumption on the part of the believer in the expectation of a miracle. By the way, if you are truly born-again, why in the world would you be caught dead in an assembly like that anyway? Your appeasement of your "Expectant God" syndrome in fulfillment of your religious duty will not leave you faultless before the judgment seat of the Almighty.

Pastors must be preachers of the Lord Jesus! They must do the work of an evangelist! They must go to war for the souls of their congregants, never taking anyone's salvation for granted! They must realize that when the focus of seeing people's lives transformed by the power of God is lost, their use in the kingdom will have become obsolete.

Our God-commissioned duty to reach the lost has been exchanged for a few hours of religious entertainment each week. If lost people and newcomers aren't visiting our churches, then we, the Church, have a vested obligation to first examine ourselves to discover why that is. We must realize that it has less to do with marketing appeal and everything to do with God's people being who they say they are- those who have truly determined to be about the Father's business.

The dare to brave the mirror of self-examination requires the courage to humbly take the perspective others have of us. How long we remain content to allow pride to deflect the Spirit's work in making us into the image of

God will dictate the opportuneness by which our impact is retained.

God is not interested in our religious programs, traditions, or meaningless weekly reunions. The Body of Christ has been entrusted primarily with the stewardship of the Gospel. It is the Church's top priority and should be the pinnacle of our focus, and it is all but lost. It is being stolen at this very moment from under our noses amidst the acclimation of wickedness to which we have so shamelessly devolved.

If judgment must first begin at the house of God, how will we ever, with dignity of conscience, give account to the God of our salvation for our part in this?

Many pastors have classified the Church as simply a group of broken and imperfect people. I realize the sentiment, but this is the description that the false Church has given themselves. This group of broken and imperfect people, unfortunately, make up the dominant majority of the local church's membership today and represents, by and large, a lost yet self-professing community.

The *local* church may be a cesspool of brokenness and imperfection, but the last time I checked, the Word of God declares that the true Church is a new creation, a peculiar people who are more than conquerors in Christ Jesus who loved us, gave Himself for us and redeemed us with His rich, red, royal, perfect, precious and priceless blood.

We've been remade as a result of His grace and revelation to us of our deserved condemnation before Him, resulting in genuine faith and repentance towards Him. Our position in God declares our innocence and righteousness before Him, and when He looks at us who are under the blood of Christ, all that is in view is the perfection of His only begotten Son- the Lord of Glory.

It doesn't take much introspection to determine that none of us are perfect, nor does the perfect local church exist, but truly born-again believers should aspire, above all else, to represent the perfect Church - the Bride of Christ, who has distinguished herself apart and made herself ready by wholeheartedly striving to live a life that honors and pleases her Savior.

Jesus well predicted the condition of the kingdom in this current Church Age. The wheat and the tares would exist together as He foretold, but if we would only realize our responsibility before Him to preach the Lord Jesus in the power of the Holy Spirit and emphasize our commission above our positions, opinions and egos, the disingenuous, in turn, would eventually part company, the true seekers might experience regeneration, God's people might encounter revival, and all would understand more clearly the objective of the Church.

At what cost are we willing to surrender our God-given commission, and why have we allowed the lamp of our first love to be replaced? Where are you, men of God of this generation, who still live by the power of His Spirit on fire in your hearts and lives? Will you not preach with out-of-your-minds passion and great boldness the anointed message of Jesus and the Cross?

The Angel of Light is masquerading as the Light of the World among the desperate, hungry, and hurting of our society while the self-righteous churches, who spend half their time criticizing them, sit idly by, stage-playing their own brand of Christless Christianity, proclaiming that people just don't want to hear the truth anymore because it's not popular. The truth is that these hypocrites' brand of Christianity has lost traction because it has no power, is void of the Spirit, produces only counterfeit converts, and is dead but doesn't know it; but the power of the person and name of the Lord Jesus still changes lives if it's administered by God's man under the influence and direction of the Holy Spirit, but as long as the Church permits false teachers to maintain strongholds of power and prestige in the pulpits of God's kingdom work, the ways of man that seem right in his own eyes will be the ways of death and destruction in the end thereof.

The Midnight Cry is upon us, and those who will truly love His appearing must prepare to rid themselves of the obstacles that distract and desist from the inadequate attempts to appease Him through the unchecked motives of our hearts as well as the corrupted works of our hands.

God Speaks - Then and Now

"We believe and embrace the supernatural concept of the Spirit of God residing and operating within us because His Spirit bears witness with our spirit, but why is it so difficult to fathom that this same God, who will never leave us nor forsake us, is capable of guiding us in the stillness and quietness of our unconscious?"

The very demeanor of our lives under the constant control of the Holy Spirit is our most effective witness because, time and again, God allows the evidence of His attending work in us to be realized by others. When our lives postulate the resurrected Lord Jesus Christ by virtue of His prevailing presence and the grace of our words reflect this sublime reality, it is then that others are able to catch a glimpse of something eternal and discover a faith that is found extravagant and authentic of our witness.

Knowing it is the spiritual fragrance of the Holy Spirit at home in the hearts and lives of those walking in step of graceful fellowship with the Lord of Glory that permeates the atmosphere of His operation, may we ever strive to burn even brighter, impacting the world for the kingdom of God by the witness of His Spirit within.

Many years ago, by the glorious beauty of His grace, God transformed me by an encounter with His holy presence that forever changed the trajectory of my life and person.

Immediately set apart on a quest to forever know Him more, the seasons of my spiritual life were in full bloom, leading me to learn what this new life meant and to come to understand how He would use it to prepare me for the purpose He had determined in eternity past.

For the first 18 years of this new existence, God allowed me to witness countless examples of man's attempt to build His kingdom. He must have shown me at least a hundred ways in which ministry and worship were being ill-approached. Apart from my time at Hillcrest, the fact that He used practically every known experience I had encountered in a church setting to teach me something about this, I was certain that God was grooming me to, one day, plant a church.

A man whose love for corporate worship and fellowship was like oxygen, suddenly found himself being weaned from the very joy he had only just discovered. From one church experience to the next, I found myself fully engaged in wholeheartedly learning and serving. My zeal for God seemed to shield me from much of the dismay and displeasure I encountered along the way. The pattern of discouragement I was experiencing, I simply chalked up to my own personal misgivings, concluding that I was the one with the problem. That, perhaps, it was all just a part of the maturation process. Jesus loved the Church and gave Himself for it. Who was I to argue or question? Through the growing pains and in consistent humility before those more learned than I, a constant effort was made above all to grasp and more earnestly know God's Word. No matter the climate, I applied myself to understand how to live this new life God had given me. So, with the support of my family, I persevered through many experiences and ordeals over the years that all eventually led to disappointing and sometimes even heart-breaking ends. Even in the face of public betrayal by a long-time pastor and friend who mentored me for over a decade, my perseverance was not shaken. Though circumstance and roadblocks may have altered my course at times, I was a glutton for punishment because I knew that the power of

God in my life was stronger than any circumstance or situation I could ever face and was the sheer force propelling my motivation. My problem, however, was beginning to come to light as God had begun to allow me to experience some occurrences inside the fellowship of my mentoring pastor's church that the heart of this saved man could simply no longer ignore. God finally brought me full circle in the journey of this years-long lesson to, alas, catch a glimpse beneath the veil of what is so often mistaken for gospel.

After all the years of heartache, disappointment, and disenchantment, I was finally moved one day to begin writing. Suddenly compelled by inspiration, I began erratically chronicling my thoughts and experiences as they came rushing in like a flood. For hours and days on end, I transcribed every event or notion related to my journey; the revelations I'd had, the lessons I had learned, the pain I had endured by those I trusted who ultimately misled me along the way as I struggled to simply understand why my salvation experience contrasted so sharply with those of whom I was in fellowship, and why my story of transformation did not appear to fit the pattern of the ministries with which I had been so deeply committed. For years, I struggled with my Christian identity, hoping to make sense of the spiritual metamorphosis I had undergone. Though it could never be denied in my heart, life, or testimony, my experience never quite seemed to fit the narrative of doctrine that these churches had so insistently subscribed to.

Though God had put me on track to begin documenting these thoughts and experiences, the revelation that was to dawn on me through this exercise had not yet been fully disclosed but would soon cement into place the missing component that would forever unlock my understanding as well as harmonize my once fragmented theology.

As an avid Bible student, faithfully living the Christian life all these years, God finally began to open my understanding in a way that altogether changed my perspective and approach to comprehending scripture. Suddenly, things started to come into focus. I admit, I can be a bit dense at times, not always grasping certain things as quickly as others, but the connections God was uncovering could have only ever been made visible by His gracious, autonomous permission. He caused me to finally see something that I had simply glossed over for years, and that was the single most fundamental and understated theme of the Bible: *Revelation*: An unpredictable enablement of perception granted by the elective operation of God. Its power is non- transferable and is not harnessed by the will of man. It is entirely an action that God grants at the sole discretion of His own good pleasure. While I had certainly experienced prior revelatory events over the course of my study of God's Word, this largest and most revealing truth destined for me by God's grace had somehow arrived to hit me right between the eyes and grant the liberating clarity that, for so long, I had lacked.

Over the last several years, God has worked in me to finally complete a task for which, I have no doubt, has been purposed for me in this life. The book you are holding in your hands is the culmination of that task and purpose I have finally found. Simple as it may seem, the message that God has burdened upon my heart runs through the very fiber of these pages, which has manifested as the fruit of my life's work to God's glory. However, it is my intention that the footprints of this my journey might fade into the backdrop, that the image of our Savior's pierced hands may manifest to render aid to the desperate necessity of His beloved Bride's healing.

All throughout the Bible, we find the accounts of God the Father speaking audibly to His chosen. For example, His introduction to Adam, Noah, Abram, Moses, and other heroes of our faith in the Old Testament. There are, however, few instances of God the Father speaking audibly in the New Testament; rather, we have the Son of God in various forms declaring the Word of the Father. In His humanity, He has spoken. In His glorified form, He has spoken. After His ascension to His throne, He has spoken. Finally, in a vision to John while on the island of Patmos, He has concluded the last Word of prophetic canon.

Throughout the Old and New Testaments, God has also used imagery in dreams and visions to communicate with the heart of man. For instance, Abram, Joseph (the son of Jacob), Pharaoh during Joseph's imprisonment, Daniel, King Nebuchadnezzar, Joseph (Jesus' earthly father), Pilate's wife, the disciple Ananias, the centurion Cornelius and it would fail me to not mention the unforgettable encounter of Saul on the road to Damascus and his subsequent revelations and, of course, the many visions of John while on the island of Patmos.

There is also the account we have of Peter, in Acts 10, when the vision of the sheet came down from Heaven filled with all manner of animals declaring God's plan to save the Gentiles and permission for Peter, a Jew, to preach the Gospel unto them.

The Book of Acts includes extraordinary events that were specific to a particular dispensation that serve primarily as a written record of the apostles' exploits during that period, whose miraculous works were enabled for God's special purposes.

Understanding that citing the Book of Acts as a means to validate the supernatural occurrences of that period for today is inappropriate. I do, however, contend that God has clearly demonstrated that He is the God of all revelation and is not confined to the limited parameters of the miniscule existence that so often constitutes our faith. My point is that God still communicates with His people, oftentimes, through the imagery of visions and dreams.

While I understand that, with great disdain, many students of the Bible oppose this position, I, on the contrary, have been privileged to experience the benefits of serving a living God, the God who has expressed and personally affirmed Himself in this way. God has a history of communicating personally to people through dreams and visions well beyond the Book of Acts, which ordinately substantiates their validity as an ordained method of expression as timeless and relevant as the Ancient of Days Himself, for those of you who should doubt. God has not terminated the lines of communication; we've simply chosen to remain disconnected. Of course, God has closed the book on any further biblical revelation to man, but the last time I checked, He is still the God of the living.

The fact that God has designated man's senses as a channel to convey personal messages outside of the written Word clearly diminishes His need to speak audibly to us. God's indwelling Spirit communicates conviction of sin, discernment in guidance, clarity in decision-making, and direction in seeking His will. Why couldn't He reveal things to come in our personal lives through the stillness and quietness of mind if He so chooses? How can Christians claim to have fellowship with a God who is done conversing? Is the relationship solely with the written Word or the Living Word? We believe and embrace the supernatural concept of the Spirit of God residing and operating within us because His Spirit bears witness with our spirit, but why is it so difficult to fathom that this same God, who will never leave us nor forsake us, is capable of guiding us in the stillness and quietness of our unconscious?

There is no arguing that God speaks primarily through the written Word, but I'm concerned that many believers are entangled in a one-sided relationship inhibited by their own inability to receive from Him. They are restricted to a fellowship where the believer does all the talking, and God does all the listening because, as far as they're concerned, He has said all He has to say in the Bible.

Pastors who prioritize their affinity for staunch conservative theology above the real-life experience of fellowship with God seem to be mostly concerned about what their like-minded contemporaries will think if they dare once consider that God just might be a little bigger than the orthodox box in which they've fought so tirelessly to keep Him. Many of these pastors and Bible teachers are so resolute about God no longer giving any new revelation (and they are correct on this point), that He is no longer speaking to man at all. It is notable, however, that many of these critics are the same pastors and teachers whose very career of misapprehending the Scriptures is principally responsible for thwarting the original ministry of the Church, all at the expense of sparing their esteemed reputations and preserving the vestige of their presumed yet undisputed theologies.

So many believers miss the fact that every single epistle of the New Testament, whether written by Paul, Peter, John, or someone else, was addressed to a born-again audience, the same group of believers that Jesus referenced when speaking with Nicodemus- those that are born of the Spirit, not those of our era who have simply failed to understand the context of Romans 10. The recipients of these letters understood what the author's intention was because they had passed from death to life, confirmed by the Spirit of God within them, not by their own might, ability or will to become children of God (John 1:13).

By virtue of regenerated man's capacity to grasp this concept, he is now more inclined to make the connections between the Old and New Testaments and apprehend the larger overall picture of the full counsel of God. However, born-again believers who choose not to know anything of a certainty for themselves regarding God's Word but instead remain content to trust what they have heard and learned from others, in my opinion, reaches beyond the realm of reason and all rationality.

It doesn't take a degree in theology to grasp the blessed hope of eternal security that scripture promises God's true children. It does, however, require a regenerated mind. Unfortunately, I suspect multitudes of believers will never take the time to acquaint themselves with these beloved truths and cherish them as a true child of God should (1 Peter 2:2).

May the embrace of this unfortunate contentment, to which so many acclimate, be ever burdened by the restlessness of a condemned conscience.

It is highly important that the child of God understands with all clarity that any such experience of divine communication through dreams or visions be subject to the litmus test of revealed scripture. Such experiences must always be confirmed by the Word of God as the determining agent in the assessment of their presumed legitimacy.

While I'm sure there are those who could attest to receiving messages from God in dreams and visions, it is vital to understand, first and foremost, that God is never going to operate in a way that undermines Himself or contradicts the nature of His revealed character.

It has been my experience that when God reveals things to us in this way, it is usually a signal of something that is coming to pass or perhaps a clarified answer to a question or dilemma that has or will be faced. Oftentimes, it will be something that will directly affect us or those in our immediate circle and typically bear the semblance of a warning or glimpse of a yet-future event that may require preparation for or even sometimes preventative measures to be taken. Oftentimes, God reveals things to us in our dreams that we do not comprehend until it has come to pass or even well beyond the fact.

God often uses the imagery of common physical articles that are of familiar substance and relevance to us to aid in the perception of His symbolically communicated messages. Omniscient of our deepest thoughts and emotions, He is able to convey with imagery and induced emotion that which is capable of transcending the depths of our unconscious and reach into the very core of our understanding.

I can only imagine what some of you may be thinking about these statements, and that's okay. I understand that not everyone has necessarily experienced God in this way, but it certainly does not mean that you never will. God is alive and desires a living fellowship and open line of communication with His children, but this gift of revelatory communication is largely inhibited by the impediment of disbelief.

When God does communicate with an individual in this way, nothing or no one will ever be able to convince that person otherwise. God has an inexplicable way of making known that which He intends to convey with those He so chooses to converse.

When Christians realize, experientially, that they serve the living God, they'll come to understand that the journey of their faith was never intended to be built upon the faith and beliefs of others. I'm not suggesting that unless one experiences God in this fashion, his salvation is inauthentic; I am, however, inferring that those who are genuinely saved and in deep pursuit of intimate fellowship with the Lord of Glory, should not be astounded, when in the stillness of night, the God of a trillion stars transcends the depths of silence to commune.

The dangers in relying on the faith and beliefs of those who appear to have it figured out spiritually are numerous. Few rarely have it together as they might have us think. I have been surprised to learn, on numerous occasions, that an individual's reputation for godliness and piety was purely a perception based on the outward appearance that others were permitted to see. The dynamic testimony I assumed these individuals to have only left me deluded once I realized that they had merely honed and mastered the art of keeping up appearances.

My point is that when we allow our system of belief to be built primarily around the ideals and experiences of those, we deem more knowledgeable or spiritual than ourselves, we limit the boundaries of our own faith and find ourselves living out a spirituality crafted by someone else. That is not to discount the lengths to which so many have painstakingly travailed in defining the framework of their vested theologies, whose motive was, ultimately, to reveal Christ to others, but that each individual must arrive at an experiential understanding through personal fellowship with the Creator in this life, on their own.

Shortly after I was saved, I had a series of lucid dreams that God used to communicate several messages and events to me that have all come to pass, including a very grave and terrifying directive to sever ties with a very close and long-time friend. I can only imagine what this one-time friend, who was more like a brother, must have thought about my total withdrawal and complete evanescence. It must have seemed as if I'd fallen off the face of the earth. The impact of this message forever affected me and the course of my life because I knew that God meant business and that's all that mattered.

In the first sequence of this dream, I found myself gazing at a dead and withered tree in the distance, having emerged through the asphalt of a vacant lot before the backdrop of a dark and dismal sky. As I drew nearer, the mood and the image of the tree came into focus, and I realized it was infested by a swarm of squirming frogs. I was left feeling deeply unsettled, sickly disturbed, and profoundly vexed by this horrifying sight. In the very next scene, I was inside this friend's home with the usual company present, and these frogs were everywhere, including the oven, the sink, the dining table, and furniture, yet no one in the room was phased by them. Let me tell you, I was. I was devastated with holy fear by this very dire and ominous vision from God.

The basic message of this dream was crystal clear to me. God was warning me to flee and never return to this place. In my search to more deeply analyze the details of this dream, I discovered soon afterward that the use of frogs in the Bible is symbolic of evil spirits.

Some 23 years later, as I sit here to recount the details of this horror for the purpose of this book, I have only just begun to scratch the surface of understanding the imagery God used in this dream and have uncovered some intriguing revelations.

Looking back, I see the dream as symbolic of my past- the death of my old life. The swarm of frogs upon the tree symbolized a lifetime of the strongholds of sin and addiction that once dominated and controlled me. The location of this tree in the parking lot, which happened to be situated directly next to this former friend's apartment, is associated with my continual presence at his dwelling over the years. The room full of people who were unphased by the infestation of frogs is indicative of their spiritual blindness to the darkness of evil forces present among them and in control of that environment, but the reason the image of the tree so deeply affected me is because God knew that one day I would come to fully realize that this tree was me. While the image of it is haunting, it is a profound reminder of what God has delivered me from when He forever opened the eyes of this once-blind man.

One of the ways in which God communicates to us through His Word, aside from its obvious literal and figurative interpretations, is, of course, through revelation, the spiritual language of its author, the Holy Spirit. As you surely know, the Bible is not only the inspired, infallible, and indestructible Word of God; it is the revelation of God's person to man. From beginning to end, the person of Jesus Christ and the plan of God for mankind is revealed throughout its pages. The Old Testament concealing the New and the New Testament revealing the Old.

The outline of events that will unfold in the future were prearranged, charted in antiquity, and archived to illustrate, through the typology of the Scriptures, God's revelatory plan for His people. The factual historical occurrences recorded primarily in the Old Testament have served to guide the Church through the tumultuous times of the last days. The Apostle Paul states in the Book of Romans:

> **"For whatsoever things were written aforetime were written for our learning, that we through patience and comfort of the scriptures might have hope." Romans 15:4**

Served to demonstrate God's illustrious and perfect plan for his chosen elect, these recorded events provide the Church a picture or shadow of things to come through God's granted gift of revelation to the elect, reinforcing His sovereign and immutable plan to imminently return for and faithfully redeem His people, His decreed plan to rule a millennial kingdom on Earth, His triumphant conquest over sin and death, as well as His ultimate and indestructible plan to secure the blessed hope of our eternity with Him in a new heaven and earth.

Jesus' reference to the accounts of the Creation (Mk 10:6), righteous Able (Mt 23:35), Noah and the Flood (Mt 24:37-39), Lot and the destruction of Sodom and Gomorrah (Lk 17:28-29), Moses and his writings (Jn 5:45-47), the burning bush (Mk 12:26), the manna provided in the wilderness (Jn 6:49), the Ten Commandments (Mk 10:19), the Scriptures (Jn 5:39), the prophets (Mt 5:17); (Mt 26:54-56), the wisdom of Solomon (Mt 12:42), the spirit of Elijah (Mt 17:10-12), Jonah and the Whale (Mt 12:39-41), the Rapture (Thess. 4:13-18), the Great Tribulation (Mt 24:21,29), His Second Coming (Mt 24:30), the existence of Heaven (Jn 6:38) and Hell (Lk 16:23); (Mt 25:41), the Millennial Kingdom (Matt. 19:28); (Lk 1:32-33), His foretold death and resurrection (Mt 20:19) as well as the Final Judgment of the world (Mt 25:31-46), all affirm His resolute support of and attestation to the actuality of these events as fact and, therefore, irrefutably validate with supreme and ultimate authority, their absolute certainty with all verity.

The Great Flood of Genesis is referenced by our Lord Jesus Christ informing us that as it was in the days of Noah, so shall it be also in the days of the Son of Man. Aside from the many parallels we could draw of the less pertinent features of this imminent reality, most notably are three specific events that took place in Noah's day.

There were three types of people that existed in Noah's day. Noah's grandfather, Enoch, who was translated and is representative of the future Church - the Bride of Christ for whom Jesus will return in the twinkling of an eye to rapture from the earth prior to the Great Tribulation and Second Coming.

Secondly, there was Noah and his family, who are representative of the elect of the nation of Israel whom God will ultimately save, the ark being a type or representation of Christ, illustrating God's divine protection over them while enduring the events of the Great Tribulation.

Lastly, there were the wicked of Noah's generation that perished in the Flood symbolizing the anticipated outpouring of God's judgment upon the wicked during the Great Tribulation as well as the ultimate and final destruction of evil.

After the Flood, we have the account of the Tower of Babel, where we learn of man's natural tendency to forget what God has done and lean to his own understanding. Man's imagination led him to oppose God's post-flood command to be fruitful, multiply, and replenish the face of the earth. He, instead, attempts to merit his own salvation through the work of his hands by building a tower, conceivably, to breach the heights of the previous flood waters in rejection and disbelief of God's promise to never again destroy the earth in that way. God's subsequent judgment is pronounced upon the unbelief of this generation and confounds not only their language, but the unity of their conventional wisdom and scatters them to carry out His command to replenish the Earth despite their discontentment and willful disobedience.

Nimrod represents a "type" of Lucifer in that he was driven by his prideful ambition to be like the Most High, desiring to make a name for himself, as stated in the passage, in his aspiration to lead and engineer this endeavor. This inference is further supported by the fact that Nimrod's name literally translates as "Rebellion".

This particular and notable event that follows the Great Flood (Great Tribulation) is emblematic of the second advent of Christ to establish the Millennial Reign of His earthly kingdom, which will bind the Anti-Christ and rid him from his seat of power in the (3rd) temple as typified in the scattering and confounding of language.

While the Davidic reign of the Old Testament is typical of the future Millennial reign of Christ, the reign of Joseph, to whom all judgment was committed by the sitting pharaoh of Egypt, (symbolic of all authority and judgment committed unto the Son (Jesus) by God until His enemies be made His footstool), who married a

Gentile Bride (the Church), ruled over the 12 tribes of Israel that previously rejected and betrayed him for a price (twenty pieces of silver), left him for dead in a pit (Hades), was revealed as alive from the dead (resurrection) and as their king (Messiah) who subsequently forgave and embraced his brothers (Israel) in an emotional reunion (reconciliation) is, perhaps, the clearest and most fitting depiction of this future event we find in scripture. Notice that Israel's forgiveness and redemption are typified chronologically after the acquisition of Joseph's Gentile Bride.

The time from Joseph's death until the deliverance of the children of Israel by Moses appears to correlate with modern-day Israel's anticipation of their long- awaited, though previously rejected, Messiah to save them.

Israel's protection during the outpouring of the ten plagues upon spiritually wicked Egypt is representative of their future redemption, and their subsequent deliverance from amongst these spiritually wicked is also representative of God's decree in eternity past to ultimately save them.

Their shielding from the Angel of Death by the lamb's blood placed upon the doorposts of their dwellings is clearly symbolic of the ultimate protection they would receive from their future yet unrealized Messiah during the Great Tribulation. This scene is also notably reminiscent of their predecessors' salvation by means of the ark during the Great Flood.

The lamb's blood, symbolic of a perfect and yet future sacrifice of the coming Messiah, provides a glimpse of the means by which Israel's ultimate atonement will be made. A means, however, that would not precede the written law God would soon establish but would first serve as their schoolmaster to lead and eventually reveal Christ to them.

The parting of the Red Sea further represents God's divine plan to set the nation of Israel apart by this figurative cleansing and redemption from their long vexation. The Red Sea being symbolic of the blood of Christ whereby they were cleansed or baptized (sanctified and set apart), but the wicked, who typify those guilty of the blood of Christ (Egypt), were judged as inferred by their subsequent drowning while in pursuit of their infliction of destruction upon Israel.

Israel's exodus, sanctification, and consequential provocation, which prepared the children of Israel to enter the Promised Land, illustrate God's general decree to gather only the elect of the nation of Israel from the four corners of the earth and bring them into the future promise of the Messianic or Millennial kingdom (restoration).

The transfiguration of Jesus is the only time Moses and Elijah were ever seen again, and their appearance alongside Jesus at the Mount of Transfiguration is symbolic of two specific programs in God's divine plan that had not yet been revealed.

Moses was a shadow of the coming Messiah, yes, but he is also a representation of the Law, by which no flesh will be justified (Romans 3:20), alluded to by his prevention from God to enter the Promised Land for his disobedience in the wilderness.

Remember that the lamb's blood placed over the lintel and doorposts during the final plague in Egypt was only *symbolic* of the blood of Christ, who had not yet been revealed. This blood had no supernatural power in and of itself, but rather, it was the obedience to God's instruction in that dispensation that secured Israel's protection and as previously stated, only foreshadowed their future atonement.

As the appointed lawgiver, Moses (the law) figuratively represents the blindness in part that will temporarily postpone the salvation of Israel until the fullness of the Gentiles comes in. This is supported by Israel's subsequent rejection of Jesus as their Messiah. Israel's ongoing attribution of heritage and knowledge of God through Moses (the law) combined with their occupation and emphasis on keeping the law has caused them to retain spiritual blindness to the Messiah who atoned for the sin of Israel's elect some 2,000 years ago.

Jesus, in this metamorphic scene, is conveying something of particularly consequential importance to these soon-to-be apostles that will dawn on them at an appointed and near-future time. Though, hearing the audible voice of God, I'm sure, certainly reinforced the message of this vision, in this scene, Jesus reveals His inner glory. It is He alone who is transfigured before the disciples, indicating His deity and total authority over the past, present, and future.

The presence of Moses and Elijah serve as an integral part of this vision to reveal to these disciples that there is a larger picture at stake in God's redemptive plan.

Elijah, in this scene, is representative of the New Testament Church in that he never perished but was taken up (raptured) by a whirlwind in a chariot of fire. Nothing complex here to note, but perhaps, in contrast to the two states of God's elect as depicted in this vision, a passage from the Book of Ephesians emerges to the surface and forefront of mind:

"For He is our peace, who hath broken down the middle wall of partition between us; Having

abolished in His flesh the enmity, even the law of commandments contained in ordinances; for to make in Himself of twain one new man, so making peace; And that He might reconcile both unto God in one body by the cross, having slain the enmity thereby:"

Ephesians 2:14-16

It is notable that James, Peter, and John, who were eye-witnesses to this event, were the same "pillars" who perceived that God's grace was given unto Paul and Barnabus by giving them the right hand of fellowship; their recognition and blessing in acknowledgement of God's will for them to preach the Gospel to the Gentiles. This exhibition at the Mount of Transfiguration provides a glimpse of God's foreordained plan to make of two, one new man (in Christ). A revelation the apostles would soon come to fathom in their not-so-distant future.

Another such preview we are given regarding God's conclusive design of divine order and intent, as well as

His predetermined plan and decree to secure eternal fellowship with His creation, is revealed in the following and final pages.

Throughout the last few decades, the prevalence of female pastors and teachers in American pulpits has increased notably as well as the general approval of the practice by average church attendees. Similarly, the wave of compulsion to usher in a more contemporary and sophisticated culture into our society has swept into the Church like a high tide, suddenly and certainly.

The idea of incorporating women from our churches into roles of service such as teaching children's Sunday school or Vacation Bible School has long since garnered acceptance and support from members of clergy and laity alike, but under what authority was this permission ever granted?

The fact is that women, historically, have been so busy serving and catering to the needs of the children, youth, and men of the Church that they have found themselves overlooked and forgotten. In the Church's acknowledgement of their entitlement to also be spiritually nourished, the necessity to form a segregated group in which to study and fellowship was realized.

Understandably, an opportunity for the Church's beloved sisters to be able to unite in the bonds of Christian fellowship apart from their preoccupation with the more domestic needs of their church family was deemed rightly deserved and necessary, but after the Church's glaring failure to address this concern sooner, evidently, an accommodation to oblige this request was made in haste. As such, male leaders of the Church likely never gave much regard in the interest of overseeing these groups too closely. Perhaps, in their zeal to right a wrong, careful consideration of the potential implications was never given much thought.

It's likely that the absence of oversight by an officiating discerning spiritual authority to ensure accountability by providing doctrinal support and procurement of approved study materials for these groups was never even a consideration, or at best, an afterthought. This lack of consensual supervision over time, no doubt, assisted in laying the groundwork for the subtle but certain erosion of the established Church family model. Based on her record of previous neglect, in all likelihood, the Church reverted back to business as usual, leaving, in essence, the women to themselves.

The targets of those with malicious intent are typically the innocently presumptuous and unassuming, which, for some reason, in God's grand design, happen to be the weaker of the sexes. The influx of seemingly relevant and trustworthy yet unvetted companion study materials that have flooded the Christian retail market intended to aesthetically enamor the prospective buyer presents an enormous concern for the likelihood of devious doctrines and philosophies to slip through and infect the tent of God's unsuspecting flock.

More often than we'd like to admit, these resources are signed off on by a non- discerning authority whose ignorance or simple indifference to sound theology should render him incompetent and disqualify him from his post. It is not that born- again Christian women are incapable of discerning such matters; certainly, any Spirit-filled individual would otherwise qualify; it's that there is an intentional God- designed order of authority concerning matters of the family paradigm, and that especially pertains to the Church family.

Once again, to the negligence of the Church's leadership, an open door of opportunity presents itself. A trusted group of women engaged in an innocent yet unassuming Bible study group becomes a target through which a dominant and very influential personality takes aim. Whether it be the slant of the author's study materials, the subtle philosophy encoded within its pages, or the compelling nuanced interpretation of biblical teaching eloquently falling from the lips of the group's newest and very spiritual visitor, an invitation into the flock has been made available, and the Enemy is looking for just such a breach.

Through this "cosmopolitan" age of domineering female persona as well as the Satanic shift toward gender neutrality and acceptance of a more feminized society, the world has adapted itself to a philosophy of tolerance and equity to a fault. Even in the face of clear scriptural exhortation and revelation, Christian women are especially at odds with and under the pressures of the prevailing consensus of the secular majority's resistance to the biblical family model. As Satan knows all too well, women, as the naturally submissive and emotionally vulnerable of mankind, make them an even more susceptible target to his deceptive tactics.

Since the beginning, the Word of God has been under attack, and its first arrow of assault was aimed at the heart of the first woman's apparent intrigue with the forbidden fruit from the Tree of the Knowledge of Good and Evil in the Garden of Eden. The first recorded instance we have, of course, is found in the third chapter of the Book of Genesis:

Satan's temptation of Eve in the garden was evidently invoked in response to something he perceived in her. Perhaps, in recognition of her susceptibility in not having received God's command to abstain from the tree in the midst of the garden directly, or maybe at some point, she exhibited a level of interest in this forbidden resource. Regardless, Satan's approach and challenge to Eve of what God had said planted a seed of doubt that undermined the very foundation of all that she knew, and after her attempt to restate the command God gave to Adam regarding the consequences for partaking of said fruit, the war was on. Knowing that Eve was now engaged in a compromising position, Satan capitalized on her vulnerability and not only boldly refuted God's specific command, but, with malicious intent, he appealed to Eve's now piqued curiosity and enticed her with the prospect of obtaining an elevated status.

> "And the serpent said unto the woman, Ye shall not surely die: For God doth know that in the day ye eat thereof, then your eyes shall be opened, and ye shall be as gods, knowing good and evil."
>
> Genesis 3:4-5

One would certainly not be to blame for asking what Satan was doing in the Garden of Eden in the first place, but that is a subject for, perhaps, another book. However, it does bear asking the question of how Eve came to find herself present before the Tree of the Knowledge of Good and Evil in consideration of this forbidden fruit. The Bible tells us:

"Let no man say when he is tempted, I am tempted of God: for God cannot be tempted with evil, neither tempteth he any man: But every man is tempted, when he is drawn away of his own lust, and enticed." James 1:14

Since this first instance of attack and man's subsequent fall, the world has experienced a tidal wave of false teachings that continue to challenge the authority of God's Word and what He has commanded. Many of these false teachings are birthed solely from the minds of those who consequently oppose the idea of a Creator to whom they must answer or give account. Society's emphasis on free will ideology has gained such traction that the acceptance of these spurious views has easily and successfully secured a foothold behind enemy lines- the Church. Subtly and persistently, a breach was forged into the very impressionable minds of ungrounded believers from whence spawned the undermining of all that is true.

The unfortunate reality today that most congregations are composed primarily of unregenerated "believers" has afforded these extra-biblical teachings to more effortlessly gain entrance and acceptance into our houses of worship. All the while, the truly saved, who look as though they have left their first love, apathetically turn a blind eye as the indifferent minority, who sit idly by and watch it happen.

No Christian should ever condone what God's Word clearly condemns, and when a religious organization finds itself permitting that which is contrary to the clear mandate of scripture to materialize and linger, that group is no longer representing the teachings of the Lord Jesus Christ. According to 1 Timothy 2:12, that includes churches that permit women to usurp authority over men, namely positions of religious authority such as that of a bishop or elder. The account we have reads as follows:

"But I suffer not a woman to teach, nor to usurp authority over the man, but to be in silence."

This passage has been attacked by liberal feminists for decades as if the Church is obligated to succumb to the overbearing personality of clamorous women who threaten the Church's scriptural position with chauvinism, gender inequality, and political incorrectness.

There are many who have contended for the interpretation that Paul was "not allowing" women to teach or to speak in the Church because of an isolated conduct issue with the women at the Church of Ephesus. While there is some truth to that estimation, the remaining verses of the chapter attest to the fact that the previous statement was not merely an isolated situation or opinion of Paul, but rather, it was given by revelation:

"For Adam was first formed, then Eve. And Adam was not deceived, but the woman being deceived was in the transgression. Notwithstanding she shall be saved in childbearing, if they continue in faith and charity and holiness with sobriety."

1 Timothy 2:13-14

It wasn't just that Adam was first formed; Adam was not the one deceived. Neither was Adam tempted until he eventually caved. The account tells us that he was there with Eve the whole time:

"And when the woman saw that the tree was good for food, and that it was pleasant to the eyes, and a tree to be desired to make one wise, she took of the fruit thereof, and did eat, and gave also unto her husband with her; and he did eat." Genesis 3:6

I've heard pastors and teachers say things like: "Adam wasn't deceived; he was just stupid," or accuse Adam of passivity, allowing his wife to take charge of managing the garden herself. Either way, these are both prime examples of how our thinking has been tainted by a feminized and disassociated culture.

Adam paid the price for hearkening to the voice of his wife when it pertained to what God had clearly instructed him (Genesis 3:17-19). Suffice it to say, we all have, and it's time that the men of God reclaim their ordained position of authority in their marriages and families, especially within the Church, and take hold of the reins as the spiritual leaders, providers, and protectors of our households as we face the greatest worldwide threat of humanism to have ever invaded civilization.

There is a reason that God's directive was communicated solely to Adam, as with all that He charged him prior to creating and presenting Eve. God did not haphazardly design this universe nor his highest creation, which is mankind; rather, the sequence of God's specific creative process and subsequent commands indicate an intelligent and intentional order of design to serve as a guide for the stewardship of the family model.

While Adam will always be held ultimately accountable for the events of that fateful day in the garden, I can only imagine what must have been going through his mind when he saw Eve take that bite. The incident must have been a fleeting yet very surreal moment in time for him.

There is, however, something about this event that happened in that garden that I want you to see.

Adam represents a "type" of Christ, if you will. He was the first of mankind, he was the son of God (Luke 3:38), his blood was shed in order to bring Eve about as a new creation (Genesis 2:21-22), who is a picture of the Church- the Bride of Christ.

The decision on Adam's part to disobey God's command is illustrative of our Lord's sacrifice. Because of his great love for his bride, he knowingly and willingly took upon himself the punishment of her sin, ultimately giving himself for her, (Ephesians 5:25) so that she would not be lost without him.

The account we have on record of the Lord's declaration of love for and promise to His Bride is the indelible quote from the New Testament:

The enlightened mind need only gaze beneath the surface of this tragic scene to capture a glimpse of this most passionate illustration of Christ, the Son of God, whose priceless blood was shed for His precious Bride when He took upon Himself the penalty of death she owed, that He might rightfully redeem that which would be, otherwise, forever lost.

In quiet reflection of these passages, the romance of our redemption is beautifully sketched and brought into view. It is the place where our perfect union and fellowship with the God of this universe reveals beyond the heights and depths of our soul's furthest reach, the ultimate expression of love. For God is love, and the pages of His Word are but the mere canvas upon which the brilliant perfection of this glorious truth has been so masterfully inscribed for all His blessed children to behold, treasure, and adore.

The anticipation of labels that critics are sure to leverage against the authorship of this liberating exposé by those who cannot fathom the totality of utter betrayal that has been propagated against them by the misguided indoctrination of the world's most trusted and sacred institution, is not without expectation.

It is, no doubt, the price one pays for speaking out against such evil. The natural inclination of those devastated by the abrupt awareness of previously undisclosed misfortune is to attack the source whereby the very basis upon which their world and its meaning are suddenly challenged and called into question.

Though the motive and intent of this exposition was never to cause harm or sow strife, I can't help but be reminded of the One whom, without a cause, they hated first. The cost associated with standing up for truth was made quite clear by our Lord and Savior; nevertheless, our passion as believers should ever bear the weight of our convictions, especially when it comes to that which hinges upon eternity.

The early Church martyrs didn't take upon themselves the torture of excruciating suffering because of what they believed and refused to denounce, but rather, for the change inside them they could never deny.

Those who preach, "If you don't stand for something, you will fall for anything," have, perhaps, overlooked the importance of comprehending exactly what it is for which they truly stand. This summons presumes that the hearer ought to join the cause of the heralder, nothing doubting, but was never the intended assertion by the early fathers of our faith to the Church.

It is my sincere and earnest prayer that the surveyors of this solemn exhortation bear in mind the motivating force for which this undertaking was endeavored, and encounter within themselves the courage to seek with eyes wide open, discovery of the revelatory truths of God's holy Word, perhaps, for the very first time.

A Note from the Author

Beloved,

I want to thank you for taking this present opportunity and investment of your personal time and effort in acknowledging the many critical concerns that have been outlined in this book. I want to leave you with some insights that, perhaps, you could take away from this experience to aid in your discernment of future observations.

There are at least 10 reasons I have concluded why so many struggle to comprehend the Word of God, and how this confusion has contributed so negatively to the image of the Church. No doubt, Christ will come back for her as He promised, and she will be a wondrous sight to behold, but until that time comes, we, as the Bride of Christ, have a responsibility to set in order the very things of our own household.

These are my personal considerations and do not necessarily reflect the views of any particular denomination or theological persuasion. In fact, I do not identify with such labels because they have all failed, in my estimation, to articulate the very substance which I have discovered to be the missing element in all of their attempts to present Christ and the way of salvation. That missing element is the wisdom in understanding that divine truth, the truth that makes all things new, is "revealed", not learned, not realized, and never at the mercy of another man's argument.

I have arrived at the following conclusions based on my observations over the last quarter century of living a regenerated life, and they are as follows:

1. The reader is interpreting scripture through the lens of an unregenerate mind.

2. The reader's perception of context is skewed by his worldview, theological presuppositions, and cultural disassociation.

3. The reader selectively spiritualizes certain passages to make sense of them and avoids others that present difficulties with the theology he has embraced.

4. The reader is uninformed about the proper dissection of scripture.

5. The reader does not understand the major themes of the Bible.

6. The reader does not discern the two redemptive programs of God's plan for both Israel and the Church as outlined in His Word.

7. The reader does not distinguish the elect from the non-elect.

8. The reader does not distinguish between the elect Bride of Christ from the elect nation of Israel.

9. The reader fails to discern or recognize the proper context and/or intended audience of specific passages.

10. The reader fails to see the typological parallels revealed in the Scriptures that aid in discerning the chronological narrative of God's redemptive plan to assist him in concluding a sound theology.

While there are certainly other contributing factors to man's inability to rightly divide the Word of Truth, these have struck me as the most foundational. However, it is up to the student of the Word of God to search the Scriptures for his or herself to ascertain these assessments and discover for themselves the revelatory truths residing within the pages of God's written yet Living Word.

"For the Word of God is quick, and powerful, and sharper than any twoedged sword, piercing even to the dividing asunder of soul and spirit, and of the joints and marrow, and is a discerner of the thoughts and intents of the heart."

Hebrews 4:12